We'll Call You

Jacob Sundberg
We'll Call You

Translated by
Duncan J. Lewis

nordisk books

Published by Nordisk Books, 2020
www.nordiskbooks.com

Jacob Sundberg, 2018.
Copyright © Bokförlaget Atlas. All rights reserved.

This English translation copyright
© Duncan J. Lewis, 2020.

Cover artwork © Simon Ackeby
Cover design © Nordisk Books

Printed and bound in Great Britain by Clays Ltd,
Elcograf S.p.A.

A CIP catalogue record for this book is
available from the British Library

ISBN 9781838074203
eBook ISBN 9781838074227

This book is sold subject to the condition that it
shall not, by way of trade or otherwise, be lent,
resold, hired out or otherwise circulated without the
publisher's prior consent in any form of binding or
cover other than that in which it is published and
without a similar condition including this condition
being imposed on the subsequent purchaser.

Contents

An Exotic Touch - 9
A Sense of Style - 27
Head and Heart - 45
Close to City Centre - 61
That's Just So Me - 79
The Soulless - 97
Bigger than Dylan - 113
Slow Cooker Saturdays - 131
Infectious like Ebola - 151

AN EXOTIC TOUCH

Alfred Hansson was waiting for the next candidate, he'd step through the door and into his office any minute now. Hansson was trying different positions to look relaxed for when the door would open. It was important to look relaxed this time, very relaxed. He would not display a shred of astonishment, or scepticism, or fear. He tried to lean back with one arm hanging down his side, the other arm leisurely clicking the mouse. Rolled up the sleeves of his light-blue shirt. Then he tried a more formal posture, fixed his eyes on the screen as if focusing hard, doing a complex calculation or reading something enigmatic. When the man would enter, Hansson was going to slowly raise a friendly finger, still with his eyes on the screen, as if to communicate 'give me a second, I'm just going to finish this first.' Then he'd look up and offer a smile, get up, perhaps look discreetly at his watch as well, as if silently saying 'is it already time?' It was a matter of showing that time flies when you're having fun – and you sure did have fun at Ice Consulting. But the main reason for Hansson wanting to look relaxed and utterly untroubled when the man walked in, was that he to all appearances was a foreigner. He had an exotic name: Said Ansari. If there was anything Hansson wished for, it was that these poor refugees would also feel welcome, treated the same way as everyone else. To be unruffled in this situation was, in other words, absolutely necessary.

Said could of course be a good kid in spite of his origins, thought Hansson. He was after all very careful to treat everyone equally, even foreigners, yes, *especially* foreigners, something he often pointed out. I barely see that they're different from us, that they're dark and swarthy, he used to say. He didn't think about such things, for he saw the person inside. He was a really good man, that's what everyone thought. Every month a hundred kronor were transferred from his account to a charity organisation. That's the least I can do, he said if the topic came up, which it did now and then. And if it didn't come up, he himself could make sure it did, because shouldn't more people sacrifice their wealth for the survival of others? He felt so grateful for all he had, that now he wanted to give a little back. That was something that everyone should do, each according to their ability of course, not everyone could set the bar as high as he did. Who knows, maybe Said had benefited from a share of his money in a refugee camp somewhere? Hansson smiled compassionately when he thought about how it would now all come full circle, Said would get a chance to stand on his own two feet, to start working and make his own money. He wished that for everyone, also foreigners. But it wasn't self-evident that

Said would get the job, since the competition was hard. Although an exotic touch wouldn't hurt.

But then there was the religion thing. Said Ansari, it did sound rather religious. Hansson had nothing against that, if people would treat it as a private matter. There wasn't much to do about the fact that Arabs and Africans were religious, you had to accept that, they hadn't had the same possibilities of education, and they were a bit more driven by emotion. But if there was anything that provoked him, it was when ordinary people, Swedes, were believers. That people, despite schooling, even university in some cases, in a modern society could practice such things, was baffling. History had progressed, taken us to the moon, given us insight into the reality in which we live. In the past, people thought that supernatural beings governed the weather, now we had science. It made sense thousands of years ago to believe that the dead were resurrected and that people walked on water, but scientists had now disproven all that. And still, still there were people – blond, Swedish people – who clung onto these fairy tales. They were reactionaries, they wanted to go back to *the old days*. What Hansson meant by the old days he wasn't sure of himself, but it was clear to him that it was a time of ignorance, intolerance, superstition and, yes, religion. But if Said brought his religion to Sweden, you sort of had to tolerate it to some degree, because down there they didn't know better. He would treat him exactly the same regardless. Also, a number of years in Sweden would scrape away most of the delusions. Patience, integration was all about patience, to give them a chance to be like us.

A young man walked through the door, they shook hands. He was handsome, Hansson could see that - not that he was gay, no, he really wasn't, absolutely not, but he could see that this Said definitely had not had to work hard to get attention from women. In his own circle that is, among his own people.

'Welcome,' Hansson said and pointed to the chair opposite his own.

'Thanks.'

'Did you take the car here?' Hansson said, gripping an imaginary steering wheel in the air.

'No, I walked. I live just ten minutes from here,' said Said.

'Oh. Great that, not having to look for parking. And not getting stuck in rush hour. *You know, rush hour.*' Hansson spoke clearly, slowly and rather loudly.

'True. I have a driving license, but I haven't bothered with a car, it's mostly a liability here in Stockholm.'

'It can be, it can be,' said Hansson pensively. 'We are rebuilding the place, hope it doesn't deter you. It's going to be great when it's done.'

Said nodded.

'Let's see... Said was it, yes?' said Hansson and looked down on his paper. 'And you are twenty-nine years old. What are you doing right now?'

'I have a communications position at Värmdö Municipality. A lot of internal communication, intranet, various types of brochures, all kinds of things. Some press queries come up too.'

He spoke good Swedish, Hansson had to admit. A lot of people who come here are willing to make an effort after all, he thought.

'It's a little different in a private company,' Hansson said, 'but you have some valuable experience. As you saw in our advert, we want someone to develop our brand. To find out what it is that makes us unique.'

'The USP,' said Said.

'Pardon?'

'The USP. Finding the USP, so to speak.'

Hansson smiled unconfidently. 'Yes, well. Definitely.'

This was going to be a challenge, that much he realised. He wasn't averse to suburban slang, he would jokingly throw in the occasional 'habibi' himself, but this was an employment interview and under such circumstances they should keep their mother tongue to themselves. "USP," now that was a word with an unmistakable odour of Rinkeby. But he couldn't help feeling a slight empathy for the young man. Imagine the journey he'd made, what he'd gone through. Hansson himself knew what it was like to be new in a country, having to adjust to new customs and hobble along in a strange language. Three months as a language student at the Goethe-Institut in Munich as a twenty-year-old had made him humble. They weren't that different after all, Said and he, both had their history of alienation and challenges. New culture, new food, new everything. He was hoping that Said had someone to share his life with, someone who could talk to him in his own language or, for that matter, someone who could be a gateway into society.

'Do you have a family?'

'Yes. Wife, two kids.'

Hansson smiled. It felt good to hear. Perhaps Said didn't have to feel lonely after all. When he would come home in the afternoons, when he'd fought his way through culture clashes and misunderstandings, perhaps endured racist comments – oh, how Hansson hated racists – then a woman and two children waited for him back home, giving him comfort and joy.

'What does your wife do?'

'She's at home with the children right now. Otherwise...'

'I see, I see', Hansson replied before Said had the chance to finish. Said didn't have to make excuses for his wife being a stay-at-home mum. Words weren't necessary. Cultures were different. Besides, that's how it was here as well in the fifties. They'd catch up on Swedish society, eventually. If not in this generation, then in the next.

'Otherwise, she's a psychologist,' said Said. 'She's just finished her training, actually.'

'Oh,' said Hansson, more surprised than interested. 'So she's...' He went silent. In other words, Said had found a Swedish wife, he thought, that's a good sign. He changed the subject.

'At the moment we're working very intently on developing a set of core values. It's the very foundation of our branding. We want it to permeate our entire business. It's one thing when you're ten employees, when everyone knows each other well and it's ingrained in the company. But now we're approaching a hundred and so we need to pinpoint what we stand for together. Your role would be to coordinate that project and then to communicate it externally.'

'Interesting. What are your key concepts?'

'That's sort of where you come in. We've got a direction, but we need to encapsulate it in a few clear points. Social responsibility is a given, of course. And responsiveness.'

'Good,' said Said.

'Do you think so?'

'Yes. Then of course they need to be rooted in something more than words.'

'Naturally, naturally.'

Hansson observed Said, the symmetrical face, the perfect teeth, the shirt. He could become a great representative for Ice Consulting. It would also be apt to have someone younger, and someone who could mirror the new Sweden. It was astonishing really, that there was such diversity in this country. People of all kinds of languages and cultures. He'd had a colleague once who was from Bosnia. Her name was Zlatka. There was truly nothing wrong with her. You hardly noticed she wasn't Swedish.

'Are you comfortable with English?' said Hansson. 'We work a lot with foreign clients.'

'Yes, I'd probably say I am. But perhaps not to the extent of writing long texts.'

'We have translators for that, no problem. But you speak English then, that's good.'

Hansson looked around and let his gaze rest on a tree outside the window. 'Do you speak any other languages?' he asked in passing, still fixing his eye on the tree, as if emphasising that the question wasn't premeditated, just something that popped up in the moment, and that he didn't attach any importance to.

'I speak Arabic as well.'

Hansson put his hands to his mouth.

'Wow! Arabic?' He let out a surprised smile. 'So cool! It must be hard. Where did you learn that?'

This was one of Hansson's great strengths, his total lack of prejudice – he hadn't noticed that the aspiring marketing coordinator could be of foreign descent. Everyone was innocent until proven guilty, so to speak.

'My parents are from Lebanon.'

Hansson looked at Said in amazement. 'You don't say?'

He rocked his head pensively, back and forth. 'I would never have guessed,' he said quietly.

Said laughed. 'Where did you think I was from then?'

Hansson raised his palms and pouted with his lower lip. 'Uppsala?'

'Yes, that's true as well. But I don't really look typically Swedish. And my name...' he said, and finished the sentence soundlessly, with a look clearly seeking confirmation.

'Perhaps now that you mention it... but on the other hand I don't know what a typical Swede looks like. We're all different. Lebanon, you say. How about that! Do you like it here, in our country?'

He was speaking slowly and clearly again and pointed his finger to the floor when he said, 'our country.'

'I was born here. But I do like it,' Said laughed.

Hansson laughed too, forcedly. They were silent for a while.

'It may be worth pointing out, speaking of core values...' Hansson started, and became more serious.

Said nodded.

'...that in this place we work very, how should I put it. We are on equal terms. Men and women together. No separation.' He studied Said's reaction carefully. 'Do you understand what I mean?'

'Absolutely.'

'It means that women aren't subordinate to men.'

'Of course, of course.'

'So, men aren't supposed to call the shots just because they are men.'

'No, clearly not.'

'Women have exactly the same opportunities. And we are very careful with salaries. Same job, same pay.'

'Very good, very good.'

Said was obviously acting along, Hansson thought, he said what an executive wanted to hear. But what did he really think?

'We are also, how should I put it... open-minded. You can express yourself freely here, regardless of gender or position,' he said. He cleared his throat. 'Or religion, for example.'

Hansson studied Said again.

'I think that goes without saying,' said Said.

'And if one were ever to get upset, then, well... That is, you could say that here we have a tradition, and I mean in Sweden in general, a tradition of not solving things with... we haven't been at war in two hundred years, so a lot of it has to do with...' Hansson couldn't express what he really wanted to get across. He took a deep breath and made a new attempt. 'So, what I mean is that we don't solve conflicts by resorting to violence.'

'I don't understand', said Said and frowned. 'Where are you going with this?'

He doesn't get it, Hansson thought. This is remarkable, worrying even. He doesn't understand that we don't solve conflicts by violence in the workplace.

'What don't you understand?' said Hansson.

'I don't understand what this has to do with the job.'

Hansson's eyes indignantly opened wide.

'It has everything to do with the job! That we can work together, have different opinions on matters without resorting to violence, it is absolutely essential!' He struggled to talk calmly and keep smiling.

Said smiled wryly and shook his head. Hansson felt that the immigrant was patronising him, that was more than he could take. Was he going to show up here and put him in his place? That was a big mistake. He had to show restraint, but what he really wanted to do was to tell it like it was, that Said ought to be grateful, we've given you shelter, given you education, medical care, we've been hospitable. Instead, he looked sternly at Said.

'I agree. Violence is never a solution,' said Said. 'Have you had a lot of that kind of problem in the workplace?'

Hansson flinched. 'No?' he said, with a blank look.

'I was just wondering, since you brought it up,' said Said.

Hansson calmed down a little. 'No, no. I'm just very concerned that everyone working here share the same basic values.'

Said nodded. 'Yes.'

Hansson smiled. He felt for the boy, he really did. He should hire him, he was a likable kid. Skills were something you could learn, but personality was constant. Gut feeling was key, and at bottom it was good although there were still some question marks.

'Do you watch football, by the way?' said Hansson.

'Not really. Well, I watch the World Cup and the European Championship. I find it hard to get involved in football clubs. It just seems to me you just choose a colour to cheer on while the players change teams all the time.'

'Definitely!'

'You know what I mean? It doesn't feel like you're supporting a city or whatever, since you can buy players. Manchester hardly has Manchester players. But the national team is another matter.'

'I completely agree. There's only one football shirt in my wardrobe,' said Hansson and paused. 'And it is yellow and blue.'

Said smiled.

'What about yourself, if you had a shirt, what colours would it be?' said Hansson.

'A football shirt?'

'Yes.'

'I don't like match shirts, I only wear button-down ones. Short-sleeved if it's hot.'

He's dodging the question, Hansson thought. It's the ultimate test, which national team you support. People could be as integrated as ever, crispbread-eating, sing-along-raving individuals with Ikea kitchens, it didn't matter, it was after kick-off they showed their true loyalty. He had even seen it in apparently ethnical Swedes, the kind with a Värmlandic accent and all, who at the sound of the whistle had revealed a blue-white bent, a Finnish bloodline, a latent *sisu* that had been smouldering in the

Swedish forests for generations. That was the kind of thing you didn't quench so easily. When it came to Finns it wasn't really a disaster, they were more or less like us, perhaps a bit more aggressive and fonder of booze, thought Hansson, but when the Arabic pride was awakened, then Pandora's box would be opened for real. Then we'd have sharia and terror and every imaginable devilry. A football shirt was more than a football shirt, it was tied to an identity, a set of ideas, views, preferences.

'But what national team do you support, then?' said Hansson, hiding his desperation.

'What national team? Sweden's, naturally,' said Said.

'Naturally?'

'Yes. You can't really support Lebanon. They're never in the tournament anyway,' he laughed.

Shit, Hansson thought. Said had managed to elude the inquiry through evasive action. Didn't it sound as if Lebanon at least hypothetically was his first-hand choice? But he had to return to the job-related questions, if nothing else, then to keep up the appearances. He chuckled a bit, 'right, right,' as if to sum up the digression and returned to the topic, whatever it was.

'Marketing,' said Hansson, mostly to himself, and then looked up at Said. 'What would you say is of key importance for a company's external visibility?'

'Right. That's a big question', said Said and sat up straight. 'If we're just talking on a general level, I'd say it's credibility. Not to promise anything you can't keep, never to claim things about yourself that sound hollow. So, it really starts at the very core of the business, to offer good services and products. And if you do that, then you have something to communicate. Which I know Ice Consulting has.'

Hansson felt flattered. 'So, we haven't done too bad of a job so far?'

'Absolutely not. But if we're looking ahead and we see what the media landscape looks like, things have changed significantly in recent years. And are still changing. You have to dare to rethink things. It's all about carefully working through a strategy based on concrete market surveys. What I mean is that it's vital to work with business intelligence. Continually.'

'Very good, very good,' said Hansson and unconsciously tapped his index finger on the table.

'It sounds as if you've given this some thought, Said.'

Said shrugged modestly.

Hansson was thrown between admiration and suspicion towards the handsome candidate. He seemed knowledgeable and spoke with great poise. He didn't sound like a fundamentalist, he really didn't.

'What's your experience in web development?'

'I've managed a couple of projects at my current workplace. The last one was when we were setting up a new intranet.'

'And that went well?'

'It went very well. You have a description of it in my application.'

'Right!'

Hansson kept digging in Said's professional knowledge, asked questions about punctuality, cooperation, computer skills, education, previous experiences, analytic ability, organisational skills, stress management, flexibility, how was his public speaking? To each of the questions Said gave balanced answers, exhibited knowledge and commitment. He was modest but in the know, Hansson noticed. He met and exceeded the requirements of competence. Hansson thought, brushed his cheek. There was a long silence. The hands of the clock hammered in the seconds. The ball was in Hansson's court, it was his turn to speak. Said waited, made a half-hearted attempt at whistling, but mostly air came out.

'I have a good feeling about this, I have to tell you,' said Hansson eventually. 'What's your notice period at your current job?'

'Three months.'

'February, March… then you could start here at the end of April. I'm not going to promise you anything here and now, but I'll let you know before the weekend.'

'Yes', said Said. 'I don't know…' He looked down at the table.

'What don't you know?'

'I…' he interrupted himself. 'You probably don't have to get back to me. I don't think this is really for me.'

Said smiled apologetically. Hansson's forehead was wrinkled. 'You don't think this is for you? This?'

'I don't think I'd feel at home here. No offence.'

'No?' said Hansson.

'Unfortunately not. I don't feel entirely comfortable with your description of the workplace and the requirements you have.'

'You mean our policy on equality? Every person's equal value? You just said it went without saying!'

Said shook his head. 'I understand you might find it hard to...'

'Hard to what?'

'I mean, perhaps you'd rather not have someone of my... well... sort.'

It was absurd, Hansson thought. Such innuendo! Would he, the anti-racist, the proponent of diversity - did he have an aversion to certain groups of people? He, the philanthropist! It was a cunning way for Said to sweep his real motives under the rug. He simply couldn't manage to sign up to the ethical rules of the game that Hansson had laid out, regardless of how much he, a moment ago, had asserted that he stood for equality and tolerance. He had only said what Hansson wanted to hear. After a few minutes of reflection, Said had realised that he wouldn't be able to live such a lie day in and day out, at his desk or at the coffee machine, despite his eloquence and competence. That was what Hansson had suspected from the outset, that something wasn't right, that this Said had a touch of contempt for Swedish society. Hansson was lucky to have spoken so clearly about values, so that it became obvious to Said that he wouldn't like it in such a workplace.

'I hope you find a suitable person,' said Said and pushed back his chair to get up.

He was polite, and in every way acted dignified – a clear sign, thought Hansson, that an extremist couldn't be betrayed by his manner, but could adopt any shape or form.

He had been so close to offering him the job, but now jihadism reared its ugly head, the hidden agenda was brought into the light. It was eerie, he had been millimetres from recruiting a terrorist, someone who didn't hesitate to use bestial violence to end the lives of innocent Swedes. Good Lord! Hansson stayed behind his desk, shocked but grateful for having escaped death by the skin of his teeth.

A SENSE OF STYLE

Jenny Sundin knew her stuff when it came to interior design. Her friends went on at her about how she should start a design blog so that everyone could get to see her geraniums and teak sideboard and String shelves with carefully considered books in the right colours, her Josef Frank wallpaper and abstract work surfaces and Finnish cocktail glasses on tasteful retro table cloths. But she fought against the idea. Home décor isn't about showing off, it's about well-being. Symmetry. Balance. Harmony.

She thought about her partner Marcel as she hurried through the streets on her way to the interview. He would definitely not understand her ambitions to change career – from teacher to assistant in an interior design shop.

The problem was not that Marcel wanted to rule over Jenny's choice of employment, on the contrary, he usually supported her. What annoyed her was that Marcel did not understand the importance of décor. For him, it was a foreign language.

It had taken a while for her to appreciate the breadth of his handicap. When they had just moved in together, he would buy a mug or a footstool or something else for their communal home, completely without asking her first. In the beginning she indulged him, allowed certain trinkets to remain for a short time, before quietly replacing them with something more in keeping with the rest of their home. He usually didn't notice until much later anyway. For his birthday one year, he had been given a hideous silver Georg Jensen bowl by some well-meaning but clueless neighbours. Marcel was genuinely pleased with the piece of junk and gave it pride of place in the glass cabinet for all to see. Jenny had taken the bowl out as soon as their guests had left and put it in a chest with other objects set aside for giving to a charity shop.

'So you don't think silver bowls fit in with our home?' Marcel had said.

It just showed how narrow minded he was, Jenny thought. Of course there was nothing generally wrong with silver bowls, it was just that this specific bowl didn't work with their look. What worked or didn't depended on an intricate combination of so many parameters that it was impossible to explain exactly where the imbalance lay. It was a matter of feeling and could not be learned. It was like with music: everyone can practice and improve, but something has to be there from the start.

It was the same thing with his clothes. In the beginning he sometimes wore polo shirts. Actual *polo shirts*. That she in spite of everything fell for him was to do with a number of other qualities which compensated for his defective taste. Jenny had understood that it was important to not confront him openly about it. Instead, she employed a long term strategy whereby he would gradually realise of his own accord that his wardrobe needed updating. It relied on minuscule changes in her facial expression when he put on something that was *wrong*. Insinuations, the occasional giggle.

'What is it?' he'd sometimes ask, when she looked at him in a pair of far too loose jeans. Dad jeans.

'No, nothing,' she would say, with a tone that made it clear that there definitely was something.

'Don't you like them?'

'Sure. They're fine. It's just that… No, forget it. You keep them on!'

Through a long series of similar situations, she had managed to wear down his self-confidence when it came to both clothes and décor. Step by step, she had made him realise that it was pointless to even try and dress himself. Now she bought all his clothes and everything for their home.

One thing which Marcel on the other hand did have freedom of decision with was day to day shopping, such as washing up liquid and coffee and he was actually really talented in this area. Of course, sometimes he would come home with Serlas toilet paper instead of Lambi, but that wasn't the end of the world. When that happened she'd say that he was sweet and give him a kiss on the cheek, because these things can happen to anyone. Nobody's perfect.

It was completely natural that Jenny would sooner or later start working in an interior design shop. She'd secretly thought this for a long time, she had just been waiting for the right occasion. This came when the town's absolutely best store, *Rummet*, was looking for a new shop assistant. It was a small business, run by two sisters, and she had been there shopping many times. She had handwritten her application on a Marimekko napkin, to stand out from the crowd. The trick had clearly worked, as they wanted to meet her and now she had arrived. It was nine o'clock in the morning, an hour before opening, when she knocked on the door.

'Hi! So here you are! You shop here every now and then,' said Louise, one half of the shop owning duo, when she opened the door.

'As often as I can,' said Jenny.

Louise had an interior designer's look. Her hair was red and playfully scruffy, her specs were reminiscent of 3D glasses and the various necklaces with wooden pendants made a clacking noise as they knocked against one another. As a customer, Jenny had previously asked Louise where she had bought her poncho and had since bought one herself. She found this reasonable, as they did not mix in the same circles and would never cross one another wearing the same clothes. Except in the shop, but if she was going there she would of course leave the poncho at home. Likewise this time. Which was lucky, as Louise had hers on.

Jenny was shown into a small kitchen area behind the till.

'I've never introduced myself by name, but I'm Jenny. Well, of course you know that already.'

'And I'm Louise. And over there is My.' My waved from over by one of the shelves, where she was standing arranging a kind of still life.

'You like our shop, from what I understand?'

'Love it,' said Jenny. 'I've actually thought for a long time that I would like to work here. It seems so cosy.'

'Good to hear. Yes, it's probably true that we have the cosiest job that there is,' said Louise. She pulled out a chair and sat down. 'But you're a teacher, right?'

'Yes.' Jenny looked around her. The kitchen was pretty non-descript, presumably left over from some previous shop owner lacking in *savoir-faire*. Lots of pine, it was quite concerning.

'Of course we need to fix up the kitchen, we haven't really had time,' said Louise, who must have guessed what was going on in Jenny's mind.

That calmed Jenny down. It would have been terrible if the shop had just been a façade and the owners themselves actually had no idea at all and sat drinking coffee in some sort of rumpus room and were satisfied. But that wasn't the case. Great.

'How is it that you don't want to work at the school anymore?' asked Louise.

'I've done it for fifteen years now. It's a good job, it really is, but I want to try something else.'

'My! Get over here!' shouted Louise and looked out through the doorway. My wandered slowly over, stretched a limp hand out to Jenny and sat down opposite her, shoulder to shoulder with Louise. She had asymmetrical hair with a fringe – the sort of hair that goes with strong opinions – and was much skinnier than her sister, and slightly hunched over. Jenny guessed that she was younger than Louise.

'Jenny is a teacher,' said Louise. 'What is it you teach?'

'History and English. For sixth form.'

'Ah, then you can teach us something or other,' said Louise. 'Right, My?'

'Yes,' said My. She was mainly staring at the table, except when she was spoken to, then she looked up and blushed.

'I was hopeless at history,' said Louise. 'Now I'd love to study it, it's really fascinating. But you didn't get that, when you were at school.'

'No, that's often the way,' said Jenny.

Louise prodded My's arm. 'Will you make coffee, My?'

'Yep,' said My. She got up and took the two steps over to the coffee machine.

'Heaped spoonfuls!' said Louise. She turned to Jenny. 'What experience do you have with work like this?'

'I'm really passionate and usually help friends when they are decorating at home. But I don't have any shop experience. I would however dare to say that I have a feel for it,' said Jenny.

She really did. Jenny had an incredible feeling for décor. When she recently bought a candle holder, for example, she knew that it *should* have been a Klong candle holder, but she still ordered a cheaper version from Store Factory. If one just considered this act from the outside, one could have thought that she bought that one because she didn't know that it was the Klong one *should* have, that she bought it, so to speak, out of ignorance. But it was the exact opposite. Was it not the height of sophistication to *not* choose the one that all the sophisticates had, to walk one's own path? In so doing, she was not only sophisticated, but also brave. It was quite simply the case that those who knew the rules could break them in an elegant manner. This applied to all forms of art, not least interior design. She explained her logic to Louise.

Louise squinted suspiciously at her in silence. 'So you don't have a Klong candle holder?' she said after a moment.

'No. Exactly.' Jenny let her gaze wander back and forth between Louise and My, who took the coffee pot out from the percolator.

'No Klong,' said My from under her fringe. She filled up three cups with coffee.

'No Klong,' confirmed Louise. She tasted the coffee and tutted irritably. 'What's this? Did you use a heaped spoonful?'

'Yes,' said My.

Jenny was just about to take a slurp from her mug, but Louise intercepted her. 'I'll take that. My will get a new one. Here!' she said and handed the mug to My who took it and poured the contents down the sink. She emptied out the other two mugs too, as well as the rest of the contents of the pot and started the procedure again with a new filter.

'Stronger, My, much stronger!' said Louise. And then to Jenny: 'So what are your expectations of this job?'

'That it will be fun. And that we'll get on with one another. That I can add something, get to bring my own ideas.'

'What sort of ideas are they?' asked Louise. She tipped back on her chair and folded her arms.

Jenny felt a discomfort creeping in. How could she get across that she knew what she was talking about? Was the thing about the Klong candle holder not clear? She wasn't entirely sure. Everyone who knew her knew that her taste was unquestionable, but proving it to two strangers in a half hour or an hour – with words alone – it was a challenge. But then she came up with a strategy. A real classic, admittedly, but it always worked. She laughed out loud and looked slightly askance, as if there was something which had amused her.

'Have I said something odd?' asked Louise.

'No, really you've not. I just thought of a funny story.'

'Tell us!'

'Ach. You'll probably think it's nothing,' said Jenny, 'But ok. So, do you have boyfriends?'

'Yes,' answered Louise.

'No,' answered My.

'But anyway,' said Jenny. 'Marcel, my fella,' she rolled her eyes, 'he's not the sharpest knife in the box, as they say.'

Louise laughed.

'So last week,' continued Jenny, 'he was at Ikea. Nothing complicated, right? And he called me and asked if he had carte blanche to buy curtains for our little study.'

'Haha, I think I understand what's coming here,' said Louise. She was clearly excited to hear the rest.

My took hold of the chair seat under her, as if ready for anything.

'And I thought, I'll give him a chance. I'll let him have a go himself. Maybe he needs to feel that I have faith in him,' said Jenny. She shook her head. 'I ended up regretting that, I can tell you.'

'What happened?' said Louise.

'He came home, really pleased. He'd got a steal, he said. So he opened the bag...' Jenny left a dramatic pause, looked at Louise, at My, at Louise.

'What? What was in the bag?' said Louise who was approaching a falsetto from the curiosity.

'Green... velvet... curtains. Haha, green velvet curtains!'

Louise's eyes got bigger, as if she was about to have a panic attack. She clutched at her chest. My seemed nauseous, glanced around her as if she didn't know where to look. It looked as if she would rush out to the toilet, kneel down in front of it. Green velvet curtains, Jesus Christ, oh Christ.

'Do you appreciate what I'm dealing with?' laughed Jenny. She pretended to put her fingers down her throat.

'But I think I'm going to faint,' said Louise. She covered her eyes with her hand in shame. 'Did he seriously do that? Velvet? What did you do then?'

Jenny laughed lovingly when she thought about Marcel's error. 'I stroked him over the cheek. Said that I loved him,' she said.

'Exactly, exactly,' said Louise in recognition.

'And then I asked him to go back with the curtains and to swap them for some white linen ones.'

'Quite, yes.' Louise nodded approvingly, visibly assured that this was exactly what every sensible wife or girlfriend would have done in Jenny's place.

It was quite simply that Marcel didn't get it, thought Jenny. He didn't appreciate that all manufactured products – saucepans, paperclips, rugs, vases – were part of a greater whole, almost an inanimate ecosystem, and that one thoughtless knickknack could perturb this whole system. Like when the 'killer' Spanish slugs came to Sweden and caused an imbalance in thousands of gardens. They had their place, of course, but in the Spanish forests, not in Swedish gardens. In the same way, an Orrefors bowl, in the right setting, lived in harmony with its surroundings, but in the wrong place could develop into a killer slug and completely take over, become aggressive and outright harmful. But then there were objects which were of no use whatsoever, those which did not fit in anywhere, performed no function, contributed no beauty, which were just in the way, the interior design world's cockroaches. Like green velvet curtains, for example. But Marcel didn't get this. In Belgium, where he came from, it was as if a vase was just a vase and a rug just a rug. And curtains, yes, they were presumably just for blocking out light from the window. Unlike Marcel, Louise understood the real point, every aspect of the aesthetic ecology and Jenny had now left a mark, used Marcel to give Louise at least a fleeting glimpse of her full ability.

'That's how it should look,' said Louise when My poured the new coffee into their cups, darker this time.

Louise had something to relate too, Jenny could feel it, as she had that look a woman gets when she is thinking about her unenlightened man, her useless but innocent man. It was a half amused, half distressed look and she seemed to be considering the ethics in talking about something that risked being highly mocking. It was a question of loyalty – did hers lie with her man or with the candidate? Oh sod it, her eyes said, I'll tell the story, I do love him after all.

'My guy…' she said and overcame her last hint of resistance, 'my guy thought that macramé was a kind of food.'

Jenny almost spat out her coffee. 'A kind of food?' Louise laughed derisively. 'We've all got our velvet curtains to battle with you know!'

'Haha!'

'Haha!'

Their eyes met and they exchanged the mutual warmth reserved for those who share a common burden, a common background. It was an almost romantic moment. How freeing it was to share these painful experiences and be able to laugh at them! Jenny's eyes were moist. She'd done it! She had united with Louise against Marcel's bad taste and taken some important points. Cheap points, perhaps, but Marcel shouldn't have anything against that, that was something he could surely offer. It was after all Jenny's career this was relating to, it was serious stuff. And now Louise had responded to the gesture by opening up herself. She also had an aesthetic illiterate at home, she too carried that grief. They were not alone in their travails, they had each other.

It was Louise's opinion that mattered, she didn't need to be an engineer to work that out. She just needed to be friendly to My, smile to her a bit, say something kind now and then. But Louise, she was the one to impress.

A new tone crept in between them, one with common cadence and they could excitedly agree on the modern home's design challenges. This was Jenny's domain, the conversation took place on her home turf, she moved easily between embroideries and lampshades and the fact that she was there for a job interview felt more like an excuse to have a cup of coffee together. They occupied this heady atmosphere for at least twenty minutes. My added the occasional chipper comment, but only received a passing response. Louise and Jenny had found each other, My was just a spectator.

'What you need to know is that we have customers and then we have *customers*,' said Louise.

'Really?'

'The odd man comes in,' said Louise. 'Even if I couldn't identify their gender by any other means, I'd know them by their lost gaze. By the uncertain smile. We don't use up any energy on them, it would be wasted. However much we'd like to help, we're not running a charity, we just don't have time.'

'True.'

'Yesterday a man came in wearing trousers with side pockets. You know, the khaki ones, functional. He came to the till with a Kähler vase. I have to say that I felt offended. What was he going to do with a Kähler vase? Eat it? Was this not an offence towards both myself and Kähler? Did he even know what a vase is for?'

'What happened?'

'I told him that it wasn't for sale.'

'Wow, what did he do then?'

'He protested. But I ignored him. Started fiddling with some stuff. 'Look, the door's over there,' I said. He gave up after a while. It just felt right. Another customer came over to me afterwards and thanked me for my courage. For not just being out to make money. I could have made a hundred kronor's profit on the vase, but I need to think about my reputation as well.'

That was a real sign of strength, thought Jenny, daring to put your foot down. They say that all that is needed for evil to triumph is for good people to do nothing. That was what made Nazi Germany possible, a number of ordinary people who didn't stand up, just did their duty, carried on living as usual. The Swedish sold iron ore to the Germans, it was just business, no harm in that. Right? Louise was the kind of person they needed in the thirties, who dared stand up for her principles instead of playing along. Not that the man with the side pockets was necessarily a Nazi, but it was true that aesthetics were connected with beauty and beauty was connected with goodness. There are limits to that which one could be a part of, both ethically and aesthetically. It would hardly make him happier, having a Kähler vase in his man cave, no it would just cause confusion. Jenny understood how Louise thought. There had to be an element of mutual respect. You keep to your kind and I'll keep to mine. Wear those side pockets, but don't try and force me into them – that's how Louise must have felt. She became greater in Jenny's eyes. Rosa Parks, thought Jenny, it was just like Rosa Parks. She refused to fall in line.

'No, I'm no Rosa Parks,' protested Louise. 'I just want to retain a kind of dignity, you know?'

'Absolutely.'

Louise looked at the clock. 'My, go and get ready for opening.'

'Yes.' My went out into the shop.

'We need to finish up. It's been lovely,' said Louise.

'Really has,' said Jenny. 'I'm very interested.'

'I just wanted to show you one thing,' said Louise. She opened one of the kitchen cupboards and took out a mug that she put on the table. The mug had a Moomin design.

'These things. We believe that these will be our next best seller.'

'Really?'

Jenny was astonished. She had always thought Moomin stuff was for the ignorant, something for all the Marcels out there. Didn't Marcel actually have one of these when they moved in together? In Jenny's world, Moomins were just a vaguely threatening character from the children's TV program. It was all so unclear. What sort of creature were they anyway, were they animals? No, trolls? And what was it about? She had fragmental memories of melancholic creatures accompanied by a distant Finland-Swedish narrator, whose voice ate its way into the psyche, took over dreams, brought on cold sweats. That these characters should become fashionable porcelain products seemed so peculiar. Were they not aimed at the same group of people who wore Hello Kitty clothes? That was what these adults did in Japan, wasn't it? But Louise seemed completely serious.

'If I had to choose one product which I think is absolutely the most classy in our range, I'd say that it's this one,' she said and pointed repeatedly at the mug.

Jenny looked at it. It was really garish. But it was a strong brand, the Moomin, you had to give them that. One had to acknowledge that it had an aura that could be considered distinctly Nordic and Nordic was really *right*. Finnish design had a legitimate reputation out in the world and what could be more Finnish than the Moomins? Maybe, when she thought about it, it actually was quite elegant, if she just changed her perspective a little. Maybe it would look good in her kitchen after all? You had to be able to change your point of view, that was a really important ability. Pride cannot replace of a genuine understanding of taste. She now saw the mug in a new light. It was actually really, really hip. The big hat on that big troll, what was he called again? Moomin Papa? She tilted her head to one side and studied it. Louise had clearly seen something in it and she was a full blown professional, so it must be really elegant. Actually.

'Yes,' said Jenny. 'I have to say that it's a stroke of genius to take these on. It's right on the money!'

Silence, complete silence. Louise looked expressionlessly at Jenny. Then she started to giggle. She pointed at Jenny. 'You get that I'm joking, right? This thing? Are we supposed to sell these?'

Jenny felt her chest cramp but she quickly caught herself. 'Haha! Of course I get it! I was joking too. A Moomin mug! How would that work? Like, goodbye to the shop!' She made her hand into the shape of an aeroplane and whistled a crash landing.

Louise smiled sidelong at Jenny. They looked at one another, staring as if it was a competition. Keep the charade up now, Jenny, keep the charade up, she thought.

'I don't believe you. Do you, My? My?' She shouted out into the shop.

'What's that?' said My and looked into the kitchen.

'I think that Jenny likes the Moomin mug, don't you think so?'

'Yes! She loves the Moomin mug,' said My.

'Do you Jenny? Do you love this mug?' asked Louise.

It was so confusing for Jenny. She had in other words been right from the start, Moomins were totally wrong. She knew that! She had just temporarily taken leave of her senses, that can happen to anyone, especially in a high pressure situation like this one. It was so clumsy!

'Of course I don't love it. I think it's hideous!' said Jenny.

'Come and sit down, My,' said Louise.

My sat down.

Louise looked at My. 'What do you say My?'

My took her chance to come back in out of the cold, to win back her sister's confidence. 'I totally believe that Jenny likes Moomins, you can see it on her!' she said.

Both of them looked at Jenny with contempt.

'I think you're right,' said Louise.

Jenny's heart raced. 'No! The mug is awful, I think so too!'

No reaction.

'That guy with the side pockets,' continued Jenny, 'haha, what a joke! Or what! Give him the mug! Maybe he'll want it. When he goes camping somewhere… that clown. What a loser!'

She looked pleadingly at Louise and My, but neither of them was listening to her any more. The clock struck ten and the first customer came in through the door. Louise reached a hand out to Jenny.

'Thank you for coming. We'll call you.'

HEAD AND HEART

If there was one thing Sebastian Lund knew, it was that you could get a long way on pure talent. He was living proof. Or, rather, really it was not so much about a specific talent as something more fundamental, more accurately the mother of all talents – intelligence. Sebastian was quite simply outrageously clever. It wasn't something he made a big deal out of. He didn't know anything else of course and for a long time thought that everyone was the same, that they understood and figured things out in exactly the same manner as himself. During his boyhood, his intelligence felt completely natural. It was only first at middle school that he fully realised that he was smarter than all the others, *much* smarter. It was at this point that his peers were knocked out by this realisation. It was then that they started making an effort to appear sharper when in his presence, then that they started to be nervous about embarrassing themselves in front of him, about being found out by his intelligent, penetrating gaze. It was also then that they began staying away from him, as no one wanted to be annihilated by such a supreme intellect. In the beginning, he was upset by his schoolmates' distancing, but his clever mother enlightened him as to the cause of their aversion: jealousy. The fact that they laughed at him as soon as he said anything was just a sign that they didn't understand him.

He himself did not make a big deal out of it and of course did not judge anyone else, just because he or she was not as gifted as he was. He had not done anything to deserve it, he had just managed to be born with an extremely high IQ. Everyone does their best on the basis of their own circumstances, he said, and patted his classmates encouragingly on the shoulder. So he yawned his way through high school and sixth form, under-stimulated and overachieving. He was, in other words, worn down by school; not because he'd been studying too hard, but on the contrary, because school was not enough of a challenge. Just like most geniuses, he was often misunderstood and many took his disinterest for some kind of attention disorder. How they were wrong! His school fatigue in the meantime meant that he did not succeed in living up to his peers' expectations of going on to tertiary education – what could university teach him that he did not already know – and thereafter he instead made decisions about his future based purely on desire. He successfully taught himself about various subjects on the internet. A bit of psychology, a bit of philosophy, a bit of law. Lots of videos. Documentaries. Everything stuck. *Trying* to learn did not exist for Sebastian, he just learned. His brain was a sponge that sucked in everything new.

One of his many strengths was the ability to read other people. He didn't really need any theories to build his skills onto, they were just there, intuitively. If you scratched your face while talking, it was a sign that you were lying – he knew things like this. He knew man's soul inside out, could gauge its depth and height and breadth. After having survived on odd jobs for a while, at the age of twenty-five it was clear that he should be working with people. There were many out there who did not have the same luck of the draw as he did, those whose insufficient intelligence led them astray. They ended up addicts, ended up lost. Perhaps became criminals, alienated. He had no formal education in sociology, but he had seen and heard enough on the internet to meet the requirements that would be asked of him. Therefore he applied for a position at the social services, decided that he had the competences required to be a social worker and wrote that on his CV. It wasn't lying, it was one hundred percent true in every sense, other than on paper. And if there was one thing that was deceptive it was papers – qualifications, formalities. Anyone could obtain a qualification, but learning? No, that was another question entirely.

Maria Gomez was very welcoming. She had a warm expression, exuded consideration. She was the right woman in the right place, Sebastian could see that as soon as he met her. She was the one who would employ him.

In a way, it was ridiculous that *he* was the one to now be judged by someone else. He smiled to himself when he thought about how *she* would be deciding on *his* adequacy, as if she had authority over him. How the *real* balance of power lay was clear already from the handshake, but he would naturally play along. Roleplay, so much in society came down to roleplay and formalities, always these formalities. But intelligence wasn't everything in this life and she clearly had other qualities. Gomez explained briefly what the job involved, which methods they used, the place that the social services occupied in the municipality, what the biggest challenges were. Sebastian nodded patiently, even if all of it was far too familiar to awaken his interest. He could do this. Disability support this and social benefits that. He tried subtly to hurry her explanation along by emitting a short, affirmative humming sound while nodding his head. He made an effort to keep looking at her, but her descriptive, kindly voice was just too monotonous. He kept drifting away to something more interesting, like the patterned wallpaper. Was the pattern rhododendrons? Get to the point, get to the point, he thought.

'Can I say something?' he said when she had finally gone quiet. He smiled indulgently.

'Sure?' she said.

'A tip for if you are working with people is to try and listen, to get a feeling. What is going on in this person's head? How can I get them to reach their inner potential? Do you follow?'

Gomez chewed on a piece of gum, he noticed this now. It must have been lying dormant in her cheek while she gave her speech. She nodded. 'That's good, listen, of course,' she said.

He continued. 'So one doesn't put words into the other's mouth, but allows him or her to form their own argument.'

'Absolutely,' she said.

Did she really understand what he was saying? It could be smart to illustrate it all with an example.

'So let's say you meet a person who drinks too much. You have to have a discussion with this person about his lifestyle. I say his, it could just as easily be a woman. But whatever. He knows of course, because all addicts do, he knows that he drinks too much. Your role in this is not to tell him that he drinks too much.'

'No.'

'Because then he'll push back, understand? Then you'd lose him immediately, Maria.' Sebastian clicked his fingers to illustrate what he meant. He continued.

'That's not what he wants to hear and that is not what he *needs* to hear.'

'No, true.'

'What you need to do is to ask open questions which lead him at last to acknowledge to himself that he drinks too much. You draw out that which is lying in his subconscious, you make it conscious, so to speak. Then he will come to realise himself that he actually needs to stop drinking.'

'Yes. It's really true,' said Gomez.

'Open questions,' said Sebastian.

'Open questions,' repeated Gomez.

'And one small detail, if you don't mind my saying?' said Sebastian.

'No, sure.'

'It's really not important for me, I just mean if you are meeting clients… It's maybe best to not chew gum. It can come across as a touch arrogant.'

'Do you think so?'

'Think and think… As I say, as far as I'm concerned, it's fine. In this forum, sure.'

Gomez nodded amicably.

'Just one more, tiny, little thing,' said Sebastian and put up his thumb and forefinger close to each other to show that it really was the smallest of things.

Gomez took a deep breath. 'Sure.'

'And it probably has nothing to do with you. But I wonder if it's a good idea to have such bold wallpaper in here. I imagine that you want the client to really feel relaxed here. I'd prefer a pale, single coloured wallpaper. Light blue would be great and is supposed to have therapeutic qualities into the bargain.' He shrugged. 'But you've probably already thought of that here and one can't do everything at once. And of course I understand that a lot has to do with where you choose to put your money in a public institution.'

She shook her head, clearly subconsciously. Sebastian felt a pang in his chest and was pulled back to the times when his classmates rejected him. But he quickly pushed away the feeling, because he knew that it wasn't a matter of him having done anything wrong or said anything out of place, it was just that he was so smart that people did not know how to act. The fact that Gomez was shaking her head didn't mean that she did not like him, on the contrary. He had been there for five minutes and had already identified several areas of improvement. She was naturally completely taken aback by his acuity, she quite simply could not understand what luck they had in him coming in. It was always like this. He didn't strain himself, he just had an ability for grasping things, thinking outside of the box, keeping his eyes open, coming up with solutions. That was what intelligence was about. Problem solving ability. He personally didn't see problems, he saw solutions. How smart was he? Well, if he were to find himself in a room with one hundred other people, he was statistically likely to be the smartest. If he was in a full arena he would definitely be top three. *Definitely*. It was at that level. It was at that level, thought Sebastian, while Gomez considered what she would say next.

'Let's see,' she said. 'I'd like to hear a bit about how you view your professional skills. Would you say that you prefer working in a group or alone?'

Right, here comes the first proper question, thought Sebastian. About time. Group work or alone, she wondered. He mastered both, but the question was whether he needed colleagues, the risk was more that they would pull him back, as a group is never stronger than its weakest link.

'I'd say that the question is not the right one. What I prefer is not interesting really, the question is what would best serve a purpose in the work to be carried out.'

'Uhuh, interesting.'

'I *can* work in a group…' said Sebastian.

'But?' added Gomez, as if she perceived an objection.

He brightened up. 'Good, you read me well there. This is what I'm talking about. Listen, get a feeling. Really good, Maria!'

Gomez laughed. 'Go on.'

'But,' said Sebastian, 'you are right, there is a but. I think that working in groups, in my case at least, is restrictive.'

'How so?'

She had of course noticed that he was something completely extraordinary. He didn't need to write it down for her.

'I think you understand,' he said.

'No, please explain.'

He looked at her with a 'you must be joking' expression. She looked back as if she was not joking. Sebastian rolled his eyes and sighed.

'Working in a group can be really creative and stimulating. But if you have, how can I put it, if you have particular abilities, then it can be a hindrance to have to be considerate. To wait for others to catch up. It can be quite frustrating.'

'You see yourself as having special abilities?' she asked, or rather stated.

He just looked at her and smiled. Then he winked slowly with one eye and kept smiling. She knew that he knew that she knew.

'Ok,' she said, 'so you're a bit… one of a kind.'

His genius had not escaped her, she now confirmed this out loud.

'Flattering,' he said. 'But you don't need to put it like that. It's not something I have earned, it's just a kind of gift… No, I should say it's not something I speak about. If others draw the conclusion that you just did,' he nodded at her, 'then it is up to them. But of course it is something I do often hear.'

'What, more specifically, is it that you often hear?'

'I'd rather not go into detail. It may seem boastful.'

Gomez passed her hand through her hair and wrapped a lock of it around her forefinger. Sebastian knew what this meant: she was attracted to him. There was nothing odd about that, he had seen this behaviour before, many times in fact, women who were drawn to intelligent men. To him. Had he wanted to, he could have slept with her; he had just read Neil Strauss' book *The Game* and knew exactly which signals he needed to send out in order to, so to speak, achieve results. Yes, he had of course already known this before he read *The Game*, the book just confirmed his deepest understanding. But he wasn't planning on sleeping with Gomez. It was unfair. That she was married was problematic in itself – yes, he'd seen the ring, nothing got past him – but it was even worse from a purely demographic perspective: if he were to use his incredible advantage every time the chance was there, which women would be left for all the other men? With great power comes great responsibility and few had greater responsibility than Sebastian Lund.

'More questions?' he said.

'I'll be honest with you Sebastian,' said Gomez. 'I don't think it's a good idea that we continue with this interview. I think you understand?'

Sebastian smiled and nodded. Of course he understood. Everything was already decided, she had already made her mind up and under the circumstances it was pointless to drag it out. Straight onto discussing salary, he thought. Gomez continued.

'On the other hand, I did set aside an hour for this interview and do have a few questions left, which I'm obliged to ask.'

'Of course,' he said. 'Let's get it over with, Maria.'

They were in agreement. The job was already his, but of course it would be nice to get to know each other a little better. He cast his right arm over the back of the chair.

'Why did you apply for this job?' she asked.

He held his chin between his thumb and forefinger. He usually did this when he wanted to demonstrate that he was thinking. He was naturally always thinking, it was mainly a gesture to show that he was considering her questions with the utmost seriousness.

'I applied for this job because I know that people look up to me,' he said. 'They ask me for advice. "How can I solve this problem? How can I get my life going in the right direction?" So I in practice already work with these cases. People put their lives in my hands. It's natural for me to want to do this full time. Working for the social services is what I'm supposed to do.'

'In connection with what do people ask you for advice?'

'Oof, when do they not? It can be everything from old friends to… well, everything really.'

'For example?' Gomez looked challengingly at Sebastian.

He wrinkled his brow. Then he leaned forward and shifted to his therapeutic voice. Calm, tolerant, educational.

'Now, Maria, I get the feeling that you have a slightly confrontational tone. This is something you should look at working on.'

'There's a lot I need to work on,' said Gomez. 'What would you say that you are working on yourself?'

It was a calm and objective question, not an attempt at provocation. It was a question he had never had before. What should he answer to that? There must be something he could come up with. He must have some weakness, and it would seem a touch arrogant to not have any answer. He looked around himself, as if to get ideas. The clock on the wall caught his eye.

'I have a habit of always being way too early,' he said.

'Too early?'

'Yes. For meetings, the bus stop, all sorts.'

'That doesn't sound like a negative quality.'

'It is though,' said Sebastian. 'If only you knew how many hours of my life I have wasted on sitting and waiting.'

'Did you have to wait for me?'

Sebastian nodded. 'Yes. But that wasn't in and of itself to do with my being early. You were actually a little late.'

He tapped on his wrist, where there wasn't a watch.

'It was another thing which I had thought of bringing up, how important it is that we be on time here in the workplace.'

Gomez looked incredulously at Sebastian.

'But,' he said and put his hand up in a gesture of peace, 'I know how it can be. It's stressful, there is a lot to pull together. Nobody is one hundred percent perfect. That's me in a nutshell: exacting but generous.' He smiled gently.

'Really... really generous of you. Yep and I have just a few more questions on my document here,' said Gomez indifferently and rustled the paper. She read aloud from it. 'What can you bring that will contribute in this workplace?' She looked up. 'You've already gone a bit into this already, but...'

'Maria,' said Sebastian. 'Now you're thinking that I would add something special and that's very kind of you, I appreciate it. But first and foremost I want to make it clear that I'm a completely normal person.'

Sebastian waited for Gomez' reaction. She would of course object strongly to this description. Sebastian Lund, a completely normal person? She was speechless, it was understandable, she couldn't get a word out. Sebastian knew what she was thinking. How could a person of such ability be so humble? How could he see himself as one of us? Others with such an intellect would lay it on thick, they would explain in detail what they had to contribute, they would show off their strengths. Not he. He emphasised his humanity. Maybe she was moved, maybe lovestruck, yes, probably lovestruck. She was silent for a long time and Sebastian realised that she was struggling to express herself under these circumstances. That was why she had been a bit difficult a moment ago, because she was fighting against her feelings for him. It was shameful, she was married and she didn't even know him. But now she couldn't hold them back any longer. His humility, his humanity had nudged her over the edge, into love's ardour.

'You don't need to say anything,' he said.

'No. I don't think I do,' she said. Sebastian shook his head. 'Your expression tells me more than enough.'

Gomez started to laugh. The laughter spread through her whole body, her shoulders started shaking. She reached out for a tissue and blew her nose. 'Excuse me,' she said. 'Excuse me.'

A chill ran down Sebastian's spine. She was full of feelings for him and he had given her false hopes. She'd been knocked over by the high. 'Your expression says more than enough.' Why was he forced to say that? Was this not a sign that he knew about her feelings, acknowledged them, reciprocated them? No, no, no! How could he be simultaneously so intelligent and so stupid! 'Your expression says more than enough.' No, oh no!

'I think I need to be clear with you,' said Sebastian.

Gomez wiped away a tear. 'Really?'

'This here,' he said and pointed quickly at her, at himself, at her, at himself. 'This here, will only ever be professional. Are you ok with that? I may as well be upfront with it now. I am aware of the effect I have on women. If it's any comfort, you are definitely not alone. And it will pass, even if it doesn't feel like that now.'

The whole of Gomez' upper body was now shaking. She buried her face in the tissue. She seemed to hardly be able to breathe. Poor her! To think that he couldn't even restrain his charm for one hour! How he wished to be mediocre sometimes. She was clearly completely done in.

'Listen…' he said and reached a hand out to her. She waved it away, couldn't meet his eye, looked down at the floor, focused hard in order to be able to look up at him with a neutral expression. She clamped her lips closed, pulled herself together and looked up.

'It will work itself out,' she said. 'I'm sure of it.'

Sebastian tilted his head to one side. 'Sure?'

Gomez buried her head in her hands again, nodding at the same time. She squeaked out a pitiful 'yep' between convulsions. 'Oh,' she said finally. 'Jeez, Sebastian, you really are something else.'

Was she going to be ok? He thought that it seemed so, in spite of everything. When Gomez had come to her senses he decided it was best to go back to the salary, to the purely bureaucratic details.

'What are we talking in terms of compensation?' he said.

Gomez smiled. She repeated his words. 'What are we talking in terms of compensation?' She laughed again but quickly regained control. 'The base salary is twenty-seven thousand kronor a month.'

Now it was Sebastian who smiled and shook his head. Would he have to rent out his abilities for twenty-seven thousand? Sebastian Lund, possibly Sweden's smartest person, would he have to slave away for such a meagre income? If he didn't know that Gomez was a kind hearted person, if he didn't know that she was his admirer, he would have taken it as an insult. He had, however, a fantastic bargaining position. They wanted him, desperately wanted to have him, so he could just as well shoot for the moon. He really had not applied for the job in order to make lots of money. If money had been his driver, he could easily have found something which would have paid him plenty. He'd previously toyed with the idea of working in the world of finance, or as an innovator in the field of industry. There he would have had a bright future, everyone said so and many actually expected that it was in that world that he would carry out his life's work. But geniuses tread their own paths. It was people he should be working with, end of story. Head *and* heart, that was Sebastian Lund. But twenty-seven thousand, no, there had to be a limit.

'Then I say thirty-nine thousand,' said Sebastian. He looked fixedly at Gomez.

'Or why not fifty?' said Gomez. 'And forty days' holiday. And free food.'

Sebastian appreciated this. Gomez was in fact willing to go way beyond his expectations. Fifty thousand. It was more than he had been able to imagine. And they say that compassion doesn't pay. The things he could achieve at this place! There was no reason to hesitate.

'Done!' he said and reached out his hand.

He stood up, she stood up. Gomez took his outstretched hand. She shook it long and firmly. Her face lit up.

'Sebastian Lund,' she said. 'This has been very, very interesting.'

CLOSE TO CITY CENTRE

It was when an invitation to a high school reunion dropped into the letterbox that the whole thing began. Could it really be right that it was ten years since Elin had thrown her student cap into the air outside Brinell College in Nässjö? Ten years? Ten? She was no longer young and it was now that this irrefutable truth hit her for the first time, at the age of twenty-nine. For her whole life, her identity had been based on her youth. She had considered older people to be a sub-species of the human race, they were separated by an unbridgeable biological abyss. It was this abyss that she was now staring down into and it was first now that she really grasped that she too participated in life on the same conditions as the rest of humanity – that she was the same genus as the forty year-olds, fifty year-olds, sixty year-olds, seventy year-olds and so on until death. All thanks to a meaningless little invitation to a class reunion.

She saw decades rush by. How much quicker had the last decade gone compared with the one prior? There was a whole life between nine and nineteen – distant memories of school desks, breaktimes, endless summer holidays – a whole age from primary school to sixth form. Everything that had happened since, the last ten years, was all too clear in the memory to give a feeling of distance. Graduation, driving license, a week in Thailand, a few Christmases and boom – school reunion. How quickly would the next decade go? And the decade after that? She was basically already fifty.

So much she hadn't kept up with and so much she would never keep up with, so many choices. Every door opened implied a thousand doors closed. Leaving her youth behind was for her like leaving a part of her personality behind, a highly valued quality, just as serious as for a singer to forever abandon their voice. She had unwittingly invested her whole soul in her youth, as if it would be eternal. But now she saw clearly: never again would she be promising at anything. It was now too late to do anything with all the undeveloped talents she once believed herself to have. All her undertakings from this point onwards would have an air of amateurism.

But it was maybe not aging itself which frightened her, it was more aging without having achieved anything, to be suddenly caught out by old age while she was preparing to start living. And everyone would see what a failure she was. Bloody school reunion!

Although when she thought about it, the source of her failure was not to do with her employment. She had a good job, was purchasing manager at an export company and earned a decent wage. It was to do with where she lived.

In Nässjö.

All the others, *all* the others had moved away. Fine, Erik Jonsson was still here too, but he didn't really count. Nobody ever thought much about him, he didn't really exist. He used the wide bat when he played rounders and listened to country music. But her, she was even popular once upon a time, definitely in the top ten when it came to looks and charm and talent and… damn it! Ten years and she was still here. There was something about that which signalled that you'd given up, that you'd settled, accepted your fate. She had four months until the reunion. By then, she needed to have moved away from Nässjö, it was as simple as that.

It was a pretty quick decision. It had to be Stockholm. Most of them hadn't got further than Jönköping, a few to Gothenburg. But Stockholm, that was something else, something *completely* different. At the reunion she would of course not just jump people and tell them she lived in Stockholm, no, it had to happen naturally, as if in passing. If she asked some old classmate what he did, maybe he would answer 'I'm a dentist.' Then Elin would say 'oh, how exciting' and give him her full attention, without playing her trump card. But sooner or later the dentist would ask 'And you then? What do you do yourself?' Then she would be able to say it as it was. 'Me? Oh, I live in Stockholm.' Sort of quietly humble. She was always careful to not brag, it was a bit nauseating when people did, she would just answer questions, show an interest in others, just shine with her friendly attentiveness. It would then spread of its own accord. 'Stockholm,' it would be whispered, maybe people would point. She herself would act as if there was nothing at all special about living in

Stockholm. There wasn't either, really. Lots of people lived in Stockholm, more than anywhere else in Sweden when she thought about it, so strictly speaking, Stockholm was the least special place of all. But still. Stockholm was Stockholm, there was no getting away from it.

Certainly life at home was stable. She travelled a fair bit, had been to most countries in Western Europe. Spoke a little Spanish, a little French. Could order *una cerveza* in any case. Surely she had learned things, surely she was something of a citizen of the world? But all that would seem like a vain escape from reality if she still lived in Nässjö, the railway town. People said that the best thing about Nässjö was that it was easy to get away from there. And she would get away. She was basically ready to go now, the only thing left was to organise a job.

She took the train there. Oh, rolling into Central Station! Oh being drawn into the hustle of the underground! People with disposable coffee cups in their hand and dignity in their expression. A man with a guitar, the case full of change. Mind the doors, the doors are closing. This would become her city. You could be yourself here, everyone dressed in their *own* style, no one else's. A woolly hat in the middle of summer, flat shoes and no socks. Oh the freedom!

She got off at Rådmansgatan and walked to the address that she had written down on a piece of paper, registered with the reception and sat down. 'Well, I'm living in Stockholm,' she whispered to herself. She smiled. Come on, get the job sorted now! She had already sorted an apartment, just outside the centre. It was called Rotebro, a charming district to the north of the city. It would take forty minutes to commute so long as the bus and the commuter train lined up. And then it was just a couple of stops on the underground plus a short walk. An hour, tops. A little longer, perhaps. But no more than that. It was a great apartment, a one bed. Slightly smaller living room than what she was used to, but on the other hand, there was less to clean. And once she had sold the villa, there wouldn't be too much more to pay.

Elin heard a pair of high heels clicking towards her, a woman appeared and waved to her from a distance. Elin got up. The woman was called Viveka Odén, she was the one Elin had spoken to over the phone. Could she be Elin's new boss? She definitely looked boss-like. Hair up, tweed skirt. They said hello, walked through an office landscape while Odén's clicking shoes echoed in time with the rustling from Elin's trousers and on into a small room. Odén sat behind a desk, Elin opposite on a small chair, a good few inches closer to the ground.

'So you've driven the whole way from Småland,' stated Odén.

Elin nodded. 'Or rather, taken the train.'

The first thing Odén brought up was that Elin could be considered overqualified for the job, which was in essence secretarial work. It surely couldn't be a problem that she was overqualified, thought Elin. She had applied for this job precisely to be sure to outclass all the competition. It was about getting a job quickly, not getting on some form of career ladder. Not yet. She'd have time for that later. So long as she got her foot in Stockholm's door, the rest would follow. Better mid-table in the Premier League than top of the fourth division, she thought. Better to have an ok job in Stockholm than a top job in Nässjö. Odén was so Stockholm. Imagine being like that, imaging having her bearing, what grace!

Odén rocked back on her chair, which had been made in Nässjö, Elin noted, they were easily recognisable. This was where she wanted to be, not in the town that produced chairs, but in the city where people sat on them. If only her old classmates could see her now. In Stockholm, at a job interview, for real.

'I usually always start by asking the same question. Where do you see yourself in five years?'

'In five years, wow.' Elin puffed up her cheeks, let the air blow out. 'Five years. Well. Here, maybe?'

Odén smiled. 'It's ok to not be able to answer that question. What are you passionate about?'

'What I'm passionate about?' said Elin, almost to herself. Odén looked at her. 'I'm always so curious as to why people move here from the country. It seems so cosy out there!' she said.

Elin shrugged and smiled.

'I once had a colleague who came from Småland.'

'Ok.'

'Johanna, what was she called… Blonde, about my age. A bit of a gap between her teeth. In a cute way, I mean.' Odén was searching for an answer with her eyes.

'No, I don't think I know who that is,' said Elin.

'Really? But oh, my mind's gone blank. What was she called? Lundström, Lundgren, no what on earth was it? She used to wear a cardigan. Sort of civil servant look to her. Well, anyway,' said Odén and waved it away.

Elin hugged her handbag on her knee. What was she actually passionate about? She went for it: 'People. I'm passionate about people. Maybe it sounds like a bit of a cliché, but I think "community" is the word I'm looking for. That's probably what inspires me the most. Speaking with friends.'

Odén nodded. 'Then you are in the right place. We're a great gang here. Do lots of stuff together, even outside of work hours. Have a glass of wine, or just hang out.'

'That sounds lovely.'

'We often do something we call a "team social". Usually at a pub near the office.'

'Ok.'

'Of course you don't have to drink alcohol,' Odén quickly added.

'No.'

'There is absolutely nothing strange about that, I hope you realise. No one will give you looks for that. Then they'd have me to deal with,' laughed Odén.

'No, sure…'

Odén became serious. 'It's something I respect, that I have a lot of respect for. There are a couple of people in my circle who are… yes,' she nodded at Elin, 'and they are good people. A lot of folk say that you're a little nuts, but I have to say that some of the most kind and honest people I have met are… well…'

'Are?'

'Yes, well,' she cleared her throat, 'non-conformist.'

'Right, I see,' said Elin, 'Although I'm…'

Odén shot up. 'Got it!' she shouted. 'Berglund! She was called Johanna Berglund.'

'Ok,' said Elin and searched her memory. 'Berglund… No, I don't know who that is.'

'No?' asked Odén.

'No. Sorry.'

'Shame. She was really nice. I think she moved back to the country a while ago. Växjö, I think it was.'

'Ok,' said Elin. It felt as though that was the only thing she had said. 'Ok.' She tried at least to change the inflection and tone. Sometimes she put weight on the first syllable, sometimes the second, with a varying level of feeling. There were many ways to say ok, when she thought about it. ***O**-k. O-**k**.* Or with a Stockholm accent: *O-**kay**-ee*. She ought to learn that now, the Stockholm dialect. It shouldn't be too difficult. Toss in an English *r*. Say *u* instead of a short *o*. Although sometimes the *o* almost became an *a*, didn't it? *Shopping. Shapping.* How did you know when to use the one or the other?

'For us it's really important to find someone who fits in with the group. We always carry out a personality test on those we interview.'

Elin had worked it out now. Double *o* became *u*, one *o* became *a*. Door became *durr*, chop became *chap*. That must be it. She had cracked the code. But there was so much she had to learn, not just the language. Like going out. To cafés, pubs and so on. Mingling. *Networking*.

Odén was waiting for Elin to answer.

'A personality test?' said Elin.

'Yes. Have you tried something like that before?'

'No. Or maybe, a long time ago. I don't know.'

'If it's ok by you, I thought we could do the test?'

'Sure, let's go.'

Odén opened her laptop. 'We use a model that splits people into different colours. There are four possibilities: red, yellow, blue and green. They represent different qualities and it's a simple way to get an idea about a person.'

'Ok.'

'So let's see. There is a number of questions with two possible answers and you reply with the one that fits you best.'

'Yep.'

'Right. First question. Do you seek out conflicts or are you sceptical?'

'Well, neither to be honest...'

'Just go for the one that is the best fit!'

'Sceptical then.'

'Sceptical,' repeated Odén and clicked the response with the mouse. 'Are you self-controlled or environmentally conscious?'

'Well. Yes. Uh huh.' Elin thought. 'Self-controlled.'

'Self-controlled,' Odén repeated and clicked again. 'Are you pedantic or sloppy?'

'Pedantic then,' said Elin.

'Pedantic... Ok, this one – are you tolerant or loving?'

'Tol... loving.'

'Great,' said Odén and clicked a couple more times. 'That was everything, so let's see... exciting right?'

'Was that it?'

Odén nodded. 'The technology has progressed. It works out your colour just from those questions. Now it's thinking.'

'Impressive.'

Odén drummed on the desk with her fingers. They both sat in silence. Elin rubbed her legs with the palms of her hands. It was so exciting, all this.

'There we go! Do you want to hear?' Odén said at last.

'Yes.'

'You are... yellow!'

'Ok. Is that good?'

'Definitely. Or rather neither nor. None of the colours are good or bad, they just symbolise different personalities. I'll read out a bit about your type, what your strengths are and what perhaps your weaker sides are, so that you can give them some thought.'

'Ok.'

'On the positive side then: you are a person who rarely starts conflicts. You understand how to control yourself, you are meticulous and usually really loving.'

'Wow! Yes. That's amazing.'

Odén held up her hand. 'But – there is always a but – here are the negative ones: you can have a tendency to be overly sceptical, you're not too interested in the environment – climate change denier? – you tend to be a little pedantic and, unfortunately, quite intolerant.'

Elin was quiet for a long while.

'Intolerant? I mean, I guess I can be a bit pedantic, sure, but a climate change denier? And intolerant? No, I really don't recognise that in myself.'

Odén smiled. 'You aren't the first to be shaken by it. That's how it can be when you look at yourself in the mirror for the first time. When you see how you really look.'

'Yes, but it's just not accurate.'

'Are you sceptical about the test?' Odén smiled smugly.

'I just think that the questions were a bit… how can I put it, I mean the options were really quite limited.'

'It's the same for everybody,' Odén said brusquely, but quickly changed to a more friendly tone: 'Can you hear yourself? That's your colour speaking now. The yellow, sceptical personality.'

Elin felt distraught. She knew who she was, at least she thought she knew who she was, but clearly she had a darker side. An intolerant, sceptical, climate hating side. Yes. Maybe there was something in that. But she was in spite of everything loving, the test had confirmed it. That was something to build on. Wasn't this why she was moving to Stockholm anyway, to develop? To expand her horizons, become more tolerant, more urbane? The environmental friendliness would come too, because everyone in Stockholm really cared about the environment. It was in the countryside that there was the meat industry, cows that chewed up resources and let out greenhouse gasses, it was in the countryside that everyone drove to work, it was there that people were intolerant, voted for the wrong parties and ate carbohydrates. In Stockholm one was *conscious* in a completely different manner. She needed to see this as a possibility rather than a threat, now she knew what she had to work on with herself.

'Don't focus on the negatives,' said Odén.

'Just what I was thinking,' said Elin.

'Everyone has good and bad sides.'

'Exactly.'

'But the funny thing is,' said Odén, 'that yellow fits in nicely to our palette right now. It's precisely a yellow that we need right now. Well, I don't mean a yellow in that sense, we don't need any of them…'

Odén became nervous. 'Not that we have anything against them, absolutely not! Lars here is adopted from Korea, so we're all for… One really shouldn't say yellow like that actually, it's a bit of a slur, you should maybe think even more about that because you're intolerant. I meant yellow as in the personality test, nothing else. But whatever! You're yellow, we need someone who's yellow, that's all I wanted to say.'

'What luck!'

'It doesn't mean that I'll be offering you the job here and now. We may have other yellow applicants.'

'I understand,' said Elin.

'We've had a hell of a lot of them,' Odén put her hand in front of her mouth, 'sorry, we've *really* had a lot of applications. I don't know what came over me, I never usually swear.'

'It's fine.'

'I really hope it didn't offend you. It was poor of me. I do apologise.'

'Don't worry about it.'

'I feel so stupid.'

'Don't.'

It went quiet.

Odén breathed in, as if to say something, but hesitated, breathed out again. Elin whistled silently. Odén tried again:

'Just out of curiosity by the way…'

'Yes?'

'How does it work, do you celebrate Christmas?'

'Do we celebrate Christmas? Who?'

'Well, you. Your, how to put it… gang.'

'In Småland?'

'Haha. Well, sort of… Yes, exactly.'

'Yes, sure we do.'

'But you don't have a tree?'

'Yes we do.'

'But you don't have Santa, do you? Because from what I've heard, Santa isn't really… welcome.'

'In our family we don't have Santa as such. But then we don't have any small children where we celebrate Christmas.'

'No, that's what I figured,' said Odén. She tilted her head to one side and smiled. 'It's rather nice in a way, the whole thing. That you take everything seriously.'

Elin laughed. 'Yes, you think that…' she started to say but was interrupted.

'We've all struggled with the big questions at some point. I can't say that it's in my nature, all this brooding, but sometimes you think that there must be something more,' Odén said.

'I think you've misund-' started Elin, but realised that it was pointless. Odén seemed to like Elin for what she believed she was and it would be of no benefit to try and clarify matters. It would probably more likely reduce her chances. No, she'd let Odén make of her what she wanted, so long as it gave her a chance to live in Stockholm. How she wished they could see her now, her classmates. What had they achieved in all these years? Stayed in Småland? Malmö? Gothenburg? It was kind of sweet really, the thing with Gothenburg. The little city that wanted to be big. But she shouldn't really disparage them because of it. Gothenburg certainly had its charm. When she lived in Stockholm she could well imagine popping over there from time to time, to reduce the tempo, find a bit of calm. Nothing wrong with that at all, if you're satisfied with it. A good quality in fact, being satisfied. But we all have different tastes.

'How many are you that work here actually?' asked Elin.

'We're thirty employees here and around twenty at the office in Oslo.'

'Uhuh.'

'Yep. So *if* we were to go further with you Elin…'

'Yes?'

'…what are your thoughts around salary? What are your expectations?'

'Gee, I hadn't actually thought about it. I'm on thirty-six thousand kronor at the moment.'

'Thirty-six thousand? Ouch. You're going to have to be prepared to take a pay cut.'

'Really? Well yes, I had almost expected that.'

'The starting salary here is between twenty-one and twenty-three thousand.'

Elin nodded. 'Yep. Sure.'

'But then there are naturally possibilities for promotion. If we can see that you show potential, then we'll of course reward that.'

'I appreciate that.'

'And you plan on moving here?'

'Yes, I've already signed up for an apartment in Rotebro.'

'Ah great! Yes, it shouldn't be a problem to commute in. How long does it take to get into town from there?' said Odén.

'Into town? What do you mean?'

'Yes, how long does it take to commute into Stockholm?' said Odén.

Elin felt shivers inside. 'What, commute to Stockholm?'

'Yes, you said you were going to live in Rotebro? How long does it take to Stockholm from there?'

Elin laughed nervously. 'I mean, Rotebro is Stockholm though?' she said and tried to smile.

Odén smothered a yawn. 'Rotebro isn't Stockholm. It's out in Sollentuna.'

An abyss opened inside Elin. Had she heard right? No, no, no. Was she moving from one small town to another? No, of course not.

'But it's an area of Stockholm! Right, an area?'

Odén grimaced, as if she was trying to think. 'No, you couldn't really say that. It's definitely outside of Stockholm.'

It was a zero eight phone number, Elin was sure of it. And that's exactly what you said about Stockholmers, that they were Zero-Eighters, wasn't it? Therefore, Rotebro was Stockholm. Right? *Right?*

'But surely it's still the case,' tried Elin, 'surely it's still the case that you say that you live in Stockholm? If you live in Rotebro, I mean. Because surely Stockholm is bigger than "Stockholm"? That's just a purely bureaucratic point? If you eat an apple for example, then you don't say that you're eating a Granny Smith? Then you just say 'yum, this is a great apple,' right? Granny Smith is an apple, even if not all apples are Granny Smiths. Surely that's how it works? Rotebro is Stockholm, even if Stockholm isn't Rotebro. You'd say that?'

Elin looked pleadingly at Odén, who listened carefully and nodded slowly.

'You mean that the relationship between Stockholm and Rotebro is asymmetrical in some way then.' Odén stroked her cheek. 'Interesting. Maybe there's something in that. Like how all Englishmen speak English, but not everyone who speaks English is an Englishman?'

'I don't know. Maybe. If all Englishmen de facto do speak English?'

Odén looked dubiously at Elin. 'I don't know. But purely hypothetically then, if you meet someone abroad. In France for example, you meet a French woman and she asks you where you live, maybe then you could say that you live in Stockholm. For the sake of simplicity.'

'Exactly! Or if I meet someone in, let's say, Nässjö…'

'No, no, no. Then you live in Rotebro.'

Elin felt dizzy.

'Definitely in Rotebro,' Odén underlined.

The word echoed inside Elin. 'Definitely in Rotebro, otebro, ebro.' She could see her classmates doubled over with laughter. The Gothenburg-dwellers, who with cocktails in hand tried not to spill any. Those from Malmö elbowed each other in the ribs. Rotebro! Even the guy who was still living in Nässjö sneered at her. Rotebro? Have you ended up in Rotebro? Hahaha! They fetched people in from the other room: 'You have to hear this!' People came in from the street, the music went quiet, she stood there alone and had to explain herself and her mistake, her enormous mistake. Elin's pulse raced, she felt faint. Her face flushed. What had she done?

But calm down now, she thought. She took a deep breath in, breathed slowly out. Tried to get a bit of perspective. It couldn't be that bad? She would still be *working* in Stockholm, even if she lived in that... Rotebro? No one needed to know exactly where her apartment was. She *worked* in Stockholm. That was how it would be. It would do. 'Oh me, I work in Stockholm.'

'Where do I live?'

'Where I live, did you say?'

'I live... to the north.'

THAT'S JUST SO ME

Einar Bark was known throughout the whole of Sjuhärad county. He started as early as the seventies, sold paper and pens to offices in the local area. In the beginning it was a modest enterprise, hardly enough to live from. But Einar Bark held out, went through the companies in the phone book one by one and built up a loyal customer base. Knocked on doors, made calls. The product range grew, the client relationships became stronger. He gradually grew so big that all of his competitors in the region moved away or went bust. He was, it was said, a phenomenon, when it came to office supplies. Everyone had a relationship with Bark's Office Goods – or just "Bark's" as it was known – and by the end of 2016, the company was declaring a turnover of 640 million kronor and a sizeable profit. In every workplace there was a photo copier from Bark's, it was from there that one bought ink and paperclips and ring binders and folders and USB memory sticks and glue and Sellotape and mouse mats and laser pointers. Whiteboards, everything. There had been two cases in the last ten years where competing chains had made the mistake of trying to break into the local market, but in vain. It was irrelevant whether they were cheaper, Bark's was synonymous with office supplies and going to anyone else was not viewed kindly by one's neighbours. Einar Bark almost had a whole complex of informers backing him, completely of their own will.

Many believed that his progress was largely due to Einar Bark's personal touch, the fact that wherever possible, he delivered the supplies himself, that he was visible in the catalogue, that he called up customers and asked how it was going with their machine – a role that became all the harder as the company grew larger. The fact was though that in the year 2017, the majority of customers still had personal contact with Einar Bark, if not physically, then at least by phone or email. Bark's Office Supplies had gone from being a single store to comprising a large logistics complex where orders were processed, originally from mail orders but now mainly from the internet.

The story of Einar Bark was well known. When Carina Alm applied for the job as administrator at Bark's Office Supplies, she already knew very well who the CEO was and what the company's strengths were, even if she had never met him in person. He was hardly a celebrity in the real sense of the term, he didn't have any star power, but Carina still felt a certain nervousness before meeting a man whose face was on the side of every other truck in Borås. It was perhaps, when she thought about it, just the usual mild discomfort which was always there just before an interview. The fear of failure, quite simply. But there was definitely something particular about the idea of standing eye to eye with Einar Bark at any moment, Sjuhärad county's own Richard Branson. She leafed through some magazines, unable to focus on the text, as she sat in the reception waiting.

Suddenly he was standing there, Einar Bark, as if she had called him forth by turning pages in the magazine. She started when she noticed him a couple of feet away. He was short, but still loomed over her like a pine tree.

'Did I scare you?' he asked and laughed.

Carina stood up, took his hand and said hello. His eyes sparkled. He had a firm handshake, not so much a CEO's as a manual labourer's. He was strong in a stocky, farmer-like way, with lower arms which no gym in the world could turn out, just a long life of physical work. Bricklayer's arms, she thought, that's what they are. Bricklayer's arms.

'I didn't mean to sneak up on you. It's these shoes,' he said and pointed at his feet. 'They're completely silent. They hardly make them like this anymore. Bought them in Germany. Afterwards I was in at the Shoe Zone and said to them, you need to get these in stock, it would be a hit. Thick, comfortable soles. The real deal.' He took his left shoe off and gave it to Carina. 'Feel this!'

She pulled at it a bit. 'Very nice,' she said.

'No, feel properly! Give it a twist, try to really bend it. Crazy how solid they are.'

'Definitely. Really solid,' she said and gave the shoe back to him.

'And what do you think happened?' he said as he bent down and put the shoe on again.

'With what?'

He stood up. 'With the Shoe Zone.'

'Oh. I don't know?'

'They took the shoes on, of course.'

He smiled and looked expectantly at her, like a performer waiting for applause.

'How funny.'

'I just can't shut up, you know. When I think that something is good, people get to hear about it. It's kind of typically me. I was in Italy once, had a crazy good pizza. The wife and I were sat there, it was sunset, my whole soul was just singing. So I asked the baker to write down the recipe. Daft, Swedish tourist you know, you can get away with it. But I got the recipe and when I came home to Sweden I headed over to the pizzeria round the corner from here. They know me, right, so I just went up to Elias there and gave him the piece of paper. You guys should try this, I said.'

'How fun,' said Carina. It was clearly important to encourage the guy, she thought.

'And what do you think happened?'

'They started making it?'

He nodded. 'And not just that. They had never sold as many before. Everyone wanted that pizza. 'Bark brought it back from Italy' and all that, they went like hot cakes. Some people have said I should have charged them for the idea, but I just wave them off. You win by being generous, I've always said that.'

'Absolutely,' said Carina.

'So,' said Einar Bark and turned round on the spot, 'let's go for a wander and I'll show you our little company.'

They went past a few offices, Einar Bark nodded and introduced every employee who was sitting at their computer. He stopped at the doorway to one of the rooms where a man was sat behind a screen and knocked to get his attention. The man looked up, Einar Bark leaned against the doorframe, crossed one foot over the other. He smiled and glanced back at Carina before turning to the man again.

'Well then, so you're sitting here twiddling your thumbs.' He turned towards Carina and grinned, turned back to the man again.

The man smiled. 'Always,' he said. 'Although right now I'm playing patience.'

'Patience!' laughed Einar Bark. He turned back to Carina again and pointed with his thumb over his shoulder at the man. 'Jeez, Måns, he is priceless.'

Carina forced out a chuckle.

'Joking aside, you have to have fun in the workplace. Right, Måns?'

'Fun? You can get that at home!' said Måns.

'At home! Haha! You're crazy, Måns,' said Einar Bark. He banged twice quickly on the doorframe with the palm of his hand and continued on. Carina followed him. They moved quickly through the office section and came out into the warehouse.

A couple of forklifts zoomed around between the rows of pallets. The background noise forced Einar Bark to raise his voice. 'I started with this,' he shouted and held out his empty palm to Carina. 'Nothing. In 1973 I was nineteen. I ordered crates of office supplies to my place, there was stuff everywhere in our apartment. "What are you up to?" the old man asked me. "I'm going about getting rich," I replied. He didn't believe me. Nobody did. But my motto has always been that everything is possible until the opposite is proven.'

'That sounds smart.'

'People these days think that you can get rich quick. But there aren't any shortcuts. It's all hard work. Look here!'

He took a step forward and reached out his left hand. 'You don't get hands like this from tapping away at a computer all day.'

There was only a stump left of the thumb on Einar Bark's left hand.

'Oh! How did that happen?'

'I've always been persistent. Our forklift had broken down, our only one at that time and I got it into my head that I'd climb up to fetch down a cabinet from the fourth shelf up. A customer was waiting on their order. I climbed up, everyone said it was impossible, but I just get stuck in with that sort of thing, so I climbed up. Got hold of the cabinet and was about to start climbing down again. I had a pair of work gloves on and one of them got caught somehow in the rigging up there, with my thumb in it. And I slipped and fell off. My thumb was still up there in the glove.'

Carina grimaced. 'Ow, ow, ow.'

'Everyone runs over to me, they think I'm more or less dead, it's a three metre fall. But what do you think I do? Yeah, I get up and say "I said it would be fine." They didn't know what to believe, the poor people were probably in shock. It's so typical of me, that is, to take everything on the chin.'

'But didn't you have to go to hospital?'

'They rang for an ambulance, but I wanted to deliver that package first. "The customer first, then the thumb," I said, but they held me back. You can understand it really, it was bleeding terribly.'

'I can imagine,' said Carina.

They went on through the warehouse.

'This is where the goods come in, through that door there.'

Carina followed Einar Bark.

'And then go out through that door over there. I'm the one who designed the flow. I've never had much of a thing for books, I've always learnt by experience. Sitting at a school desk all day? No chance! Simple common sense, that's my tune. And now when the experts come here to teach me how to do things, they see that I've had it right all along. It's too much! They spend years at university just to work out something that I'd already figured in the eighties. Supply chain management and all that nonsense. There's too much talking these days.'

They completed the tour of the warehouse in a few minutes and went back into the office area via another door. New corridors, new faces behind screens. Einar Bark slowed down and stopped, nodded to a framed newspaper article on the wall. Carina looked at it. Einar Bark looked at Carina.

'From the twentieth anniversary. The council's chief spokesperson was here,' he said.

She scanned the article. 'Impressive,' she said and turned back to him.

'Did you manage to read it all?'

'No-o, I didn't.'

'Read to the end!'

Carina read the text out loud. Einar Bark's lips moved in time with hers when the article got to the final sentence: 'and none of this would have been possible without the founder and driving force, Einar Bark.' Carina looked up and appeared impressed. Einar Bark waved a hand dismissively.

'Ach,' he laughed. 'That old article. It must have been a slow news day or something! Let's go sit in my office.'

They each sat down on a club chair with a coffee table between them in Einar Bark's office. On the table were two cinnamon buns on top of napkins.

'It's important that you feel at home here. Dig in!' he said. 'Coffee?' He poured each of them a cup from a thermos, tore off half the bun in one bite, as if with his neck muscles.

'It's really great to meet you,' he said between bites. 'I love meeting new people, that's just the way I am.'

'Likewise. Thank you.'

'I don't really know how else you can be. People! People have always been front and centre for me. Jeez, the number of people I've met down the years. And I remember all of them. There's something in here, it just sticks,' he said and tapped a finger against his temple. 'If I see a face I recognise in town, it just clicks, I know the name straight away. I have a strange ability I think, some form of affliction I drag around. But now we should be talking about you, Carina!'

'Yes, right. Where do you want to begin?' she said.

He swept together a few crumbs with the underside of his hand, brushed them down into the thumbless left hand, stood up from the chair, took two steps over to the waste paper basket and dropped the crumbs into it.

'Please excuse me if I'm overly inquisitive, but people interest me, you understand, they always have,' he said and sat down. 'I want to know everything! What do you like?'

'What do I like?'

'Yes, what do you like doing?'

'Yes, well... I don't know, I like travelling.'

Einar Bark held up an index finger to silence her. 'Have you been to Rhodes?'

'No, not Rhodes specifically, but Crete...'

'You need to go! My wife and I have always said, if we were to move abroad somewhere, it would be to Rhodes. I'm basically one of the old school who believe that you can't beat the summer in Sweden. That's just how it is, the Swedish summer is superior, but at the same time there are eleven other months in the year. We've really fallen in love with Rhodes. Eva is completely nuts about the wine down there, there's something special about drinking it when you're actually there. I mean, not that she drinks too much, absolutely not, but you know, there'll be one glass with dinner and maybe one more afterwards on the balcony. No, no, we drink when we eat, both Eva and I. And the people too! A totally different culture, a different attitude. Just sitting looking at them, letting the hours pass, I always say it's an art that has been lost in this country, just sitting and watching people. But at the same time, it would take a lot to leave this country permanently. It would have to be when I'm retired in any case. *If* I retire. People say to me, "Hey Einar, you'll never stop working." And as it feels now, they might be right. But when I relax then I really relax. We've been to Croatia and to Italy and Majorcs and so on, and that's all lovely and pleasant, but when we got to Rhodes, we just looked at each other, Eva and I. It was as if we both said, "We've found it." Of course, it's a personal thing, some people like Spain. Or Thailand. But I have to say, Asia has never tempted me. Sticky wok dishes and coconut milk, no chance. Sit on a plane for twelve hours just for a slightly worse time than you'd have in the Mediterranean. Nope.'

He shook his head. Carina realised that it was her turn to speak.

'Yes, but travelling is fun. And I like painting.'

Einar Bark looked confusedly at her.

'Speaking of things I enjoy,' she added with a forced laugh.

'Aha! An artist no less! I have to say, what separates us from animals is the ability to appreciate art. I can get all teary eyed just from walking into a gallery. I guess I had something of an ambition in my youth to paint, but it never reached more than amateur level, high amateur level certainly, but then all this with the company and the family happened. I shouldn't complain. Now I'm mainly a consumer of art. I like that Dutchman.'

'Rembrandt?'

'No. What's he called… the guy with the ear.'

'Van Gogh.'

'Van Gogh! Wonderful drawings, wonderful drawings.'

'He is good,' said Carina.

'But tell me then,' said Einar Bark. 'What is it you paint?'

'It's mainly watercolours, the odd portrait and so on. Nothing sophisticated.'

'But still! I always say that everyone can learn to be really good at something. "That's easy for you to say," people tell me. "It's so easy for you." But they're wrong, I'm not more gifted than others, that's a misconception. It's become gospel out there, "him with the talents," as if I hadn't worked hard. I'll tell you now that I've worked really hard to get where I am today. So keep working at it, that's the tip I can give you!'

'Yes. But I don't have great ambitions with painting. I do it to relax.'

Einar Barker closed his eyes. 'Mmm. To relax, exactly.' He opened his eyes again and leaned forward. His voice became more intimate.

'Lots of people think I'm just a very, very successful businessman.'

Carina nodded.

'I mean, how would you describe me?'

'Well…'

'Be honest!'

'Yes, well, pretty much. A… skilful entrepreneur.'

'A mogul, yes. A shrewd businessman. But that's a far too simple view. I've got a completely different side too. There's something else which characterises me, possibly even more. In any case for those who know me.'

'Really?'

'Yes… no, forget it actually,' he said and looked down at the table. 'This isn't the place.'

'Go on, tell me!'

He reluctantly opened his mouth. Hesitated. 'I write. It's my true passion. At some point I'm sure I'll publish something, but at the same time… I'm responsible for the company. Mainly poetry. But I don't want to bore you with all this!'

'No?'

He shook his head. 'No, no, no,' he said, at the same time as his hand almost invisibly felt in the file that was stood leaning against his chair.

'But now I'm curious,' said Carina without conviction.

'It would be this one, then,' he said and just at that moment took a sheet of paper out of the file. He cleared his throat. Carina leaned forward. He read:

A stone. A black stone
Big as a mountain
It blocked the way
Everyone was astonished
Who can dislodge the stone?
A character approached
His face like flint
Followed by cinders
He. He can dislodge the stone
Everyone was astonished
The stone turned to sand

Carina waited, thought that there would be more. When he looked up she said 'Great!'

'Not exactly one of my best ones. I wrote it when I was building the warehouse. There were lots of hurdles. They didn't want a warehouse here.'

'Who?'

'The council. They wanted to have homes here.'

'But you didn't give in! Well done.'

'And twenty years later they celebrated with us. Then it suited them!'

Einar Bark shunted the poem over the table towards Carina. 'Toss it in the waste paper basket, please. I'm tired of it. That's the original, I don't have copies.'

'But then you shouldn't do that, surely?'

'Yes, just chuck it. Or do what you want with it. You can keep it, though God knows what you'd want that old thing for.'

She took the piece of paper and carefully put it into her bag. 'Are you sure?'

'Yes, I don't want to see it!'

'Thank you!'

'If it can give you some pleasure.' Einar Bark shrugged modestly. 'It's often the way. People think that I don't see the value in my own work. "But you write so well." Sure, but take it then if you think it gives you something. Personally I'm tired of it. I've written so many poems that it's tough to keep track of them all. But of course, if that's what people want, then perhaps I should publish something.'

Carina agreed. 'Absolutely, I think so.'

She lifted her coffee, remembered that she'd finished it and put it down again.

'Refill?' asked Einar Bark and grasped the pot.

'No, it's fine.'

'Now I need to ask you: how does it feel to actually be here? To see all this from the inside?'

'Well, it feels good. It was fun looking around.'

'It is a bit of a jack of all trades job, that was clear from the advert, right?' he said.

'Yes, that's how I understood it.'

'Answering the phone, dealing with returns and so on. We very rarely get complaints, but it does happen occasionally. And then the important thing is to really exceed their expectations. Service, service, service. You'll of course have others around you who work with this stuff. What is it you do at the moment?'

'I'm unemployed, actually. Or "between two jobs," as they say. I was let go when Steens moved their office to Stockholm.'

'Terrible, terrible.' Einar Bark sighed deeply. 'There is something sick with this Stockholm syndrome.'

'Stockholm syndrome?'

'Yes. This thing with everyone moving their offices there. It's tragic. What does Stockholm have that Borås does not? Not everyone can live in Stockholm, surely?'

Carina was about to correct him but didn't want to cause unnecessary friction.

'So I've been unemployed for about a month,' she said instead.

'So that means you would be able to start soon?'

'Yes.'

Einar Bark sat up in his chair. Something in his expression changed. 'Attention to detail and due care are extra important in this role. Being interested in people. Do these things apply to you?'

His frivolous tone had vanished. Now he was Bark the CEO, with the demeanour one could expect of a real business leader.

'Yes, definitely,' said Carina. Einar Bark's rapid metamorphosis meant that her voice had become unsteady. 'I'm always curious to hear about other people.'

'Ok then,' said Einar Bark, still with the director's voice. 'Where do my wife and I normally go on holiday?'

'How do you mean?'

'Well, I'm asking where my wife and I go on holiday?'

'To Rhodes. You said so yourself.'

Einar Bark smiled. 'Correct. And what is my wife called?'

'Wasn't it… Eva?'

He nodded. 'Let's up the difficulty level a bit.'

Carina swallowed hard. Had he bored her with those stories just to test her? What else had he told her? They drank wine and went to Thailand too, him and the wife. Or was it that they never went there? What was it, had he worked as a shoe salesman at some point or what was that one about? Oh the hell she was trapped in. It was like a surprise exam and she had just smiled and nodded, not bothered about Einar Bark's destiny and adventures.

'Ok. Who wrote the article? The one you read.'

'Borås Courrier.'

'Yes, but what was the name of the reporter?'

'It wasn't mentioned. There was no byline,' said Carina.

Einar Bark lit up. 'Very good! There was no byline.'

'A trick question then,' said Carina and smiled.

'You always need a trick question,' said Einar Bark. He folded his arms. 'What was the name of the pizza chef who used my Italian recipe?'

Carina searched in her head. What are pizza chefs normally called? Manuel? Josef? No.

'José,' she guessed.

He shook his head. 'Elias is his name. A really good guy.'

'Elias. That's it,' said Carina, as if she now remembered.

Einar Bark went quiet and looked at her. He hummed to himself. 'But still. Three out of four points. That's the best so far.'

'Best so far? Do you ask everyone the same questions?'

'The same questions. Rhodes, the wife, the newspaper article, the pizza chef.'

'Amazing,' said Carina.

Einar Bark rubbed his face. 'There is one quality I value really highly,' he said.

'Ok.'

'Honesty. I want those who work with me to be one hundred percent honest with me.'

'Of course.'

'Now I want you to tell me what you think about the poem. Really.'

Carina hesitated. 'Completely honestly?'

'Be brutally truthful,' he said.

Einar Bark smiled. Carina interpreted his smile as meaning that the whole poetry thing had just been a test, maybe to see if her politeness won over her honesty. She thought that he was now showing a level-headed self, free of frivolity. He didn't write poems at all, he just enjoyed messing around to test his applicants. Pretty imaginative, she gave him that and surely she'd rather have a crafty old dog for a boss than a conceited dreamer? If it was honesty he wanted, then it was honesty he'd get, she thought.

'Ok.' Carina took a deep breath. 'I thought that it was genuinely painful. You should probably stick to office supplies, you seem to be really good at that.'

Einar Bark's smile vanished, but Carina didn't notice, carried away with the powerful release of honesty.

'I was actually worried for a moment,' she continued, 'that you really meant all that stuff seriously. That you genuinely believed that…'

Carina went silent when she looked up at Einar Bark, who was trying to hold back his feelings. His eyes were red and moist, his posture slouched. He was breathing loudly through his nose. Visibly beaten, he threw up his arm and pointed to the door.

'Please. Leave. Now.'

THE SOULLESS

Doers! Oh, how I hate doers. I hate them, those proud, upright, eternally smiling, indefatigable, self-satisfied types. These people who only see possibilities, never hindrances, who don't doubt themselves, who have no inner darkness, no hidden depths, only surface and lots and lots of self-belief. Oh, how I hate them. They are so fleet of foot, 'each kilo weighs seven hundred grams,' although they've never read the poem. They get their life philosophy from other doers, those who have done even more than themselves, have become rich from saying that everyone can, everyone has it in them, everyone can become the best. They want to go forward, regardless of direction, toward heaven or hell makes no difference, forwards, now, do, do, do. To succeed, that's their motto, but at what is unimportant.

It is, I admit, the doers who get things done. For this they receive the favour of the common man, our adulation, for they act – but only without thinking, without considering the consequences of their actions, without acknowledging that the moronic, pitifully small fruit of their labour is negligible, meaningless. If they thought about it, they would see the meaninglessness in acting. There is a devilish logic in this: action is inversely proportional to wisdom. It is the doers who drive society forward while we thinkers shake our heads, full of opinions but paralysed by our navel gazing.

And who am I to call myself a thinker, you wonder? I'm nobody at all. Unemployed, idle, someone who does not take action, a parasite on society, an abstainer, a disgrace. But is this about me? No, it is about them, about those who count. It has always been about them and will always be about them. Doers think that everyone loves them, that's why they are completely transparent. They don't have anything to hide, they only have one persona, they are just as private in public as they are public in private. You can hear them unselfconsciously talking on the phone in the bus, about feelings (as if they had any), about business, about all the things which should be whispered in confidence. They are democratic in that sense, because they treat everyone in the same manner, even in those cases where one may have wished that they would adjust their tone to, say, a five year old, or a terminal cancer patient. I'll give them that. They are themselves through and through, because they only have one dimension.

But we thinkers are also democratic. We hate everyone equally, including ourselves. Loving and hating oneself are just two sides of the same coin. Thinkers and doers, we are all obsessed with ourselves, with our worth or lack thereof, with our greatness or our depravity. The difference is that we, the thinkers, have the truth and they have happiness, because ignorance is the key to bliss. But I'd never swap truth for happiness. Never.

Of all the doers, the salesperson is the foremost. He embodies soullessness, he is the greatest of all inhumans, robotesque. That was why I applied for the job. I wanted, as a part of my search for the truth, to find the root of the salesperson's being. Are they already soulless from the start, is that a prerequisite in itself for becoming a salesperson, or do they lose their souls through exercising their occupation? I wanted to know if this identity is unchangeable or whether a salesperson can get their soul back – and could I give up my soul if I became a salesman? Thus applying for a job in sales came purely from an academic point of view, a fascination as to how low a person can sink. The unemployed may have reached the bottom, but the salesperson has bored through it, down to the consuming magma below. I therefore was setting out on my mission with my own soul at risk.

I have studied them for years, so I knew in theory how to act. I'd even practiced their way of walking – not, of course, in reality, but in my mind – the straight back, the relaxed but dignified step, the smile, above all the smile, the superior but fraudulently benevolent smile. It was the glint in the eye that I struggled with above all, the salesperson's voracious look, the obsession with mammon. I wouldn't say that I actually lied on my CV, but I did, how can I put it... stretch it a little, to be sure to get an interview. My plan worked. He received me, Martin Frisk, the salesman's salesman, with a casual handshake, as if we were friends, and a 'How's it going?' with an obvious disinterest in the answer. I felt the disdain. Oh, how I felt the disdain for him and for a few seconds I didn't think I would be capable of going through with the charade. But with science in mind – I was after all doing this in the name of science and science alone – I managed to show restraint. He didn't notice anything, salespeople notice nothing, they think that they are people people but they aren't, they don't even know themselves. And still he tried to get into my soul, he who is missing one himself, through using my first name. My *name*! *My* name! He used it like a new toy he'd bought with his sales commission. Have a seat Fredrik, what weather, Fredrik, coffee, Fredrik? He smelled of cologne, the bastard, cologne and posh tobacco and he turned my name into a harlot. It was of course a power play, I understood that, so I made an effort to use his name every time he used mine. Funny that you happen to ask Martin, I have to be honest, Martin, I... But every time I did, it felt strange to me, as if it was my own self that I was giving away piece by piece, instead of conquering his. For him it seemed apparently quite natural. Maybe it's a given – he who doesn't know any person in a meaningful way, knows every person just as well and calls each one by name.

It was video conference technology that I was to sell. Not just straightforward retail sales, insisted Frisk, no, here it was real business relationships that counted. Major, serious stuff. Video conference facilities, made to minimise the need for actual meetings, to the gain of virtual ones. There were large amounts of money to be saved on travel by their clients. Why cross half the country, or half of Europe, when you can each sit in your own room with a large screen on the wall? It was wonderful; longer term you'd be able to reduce the number of human interactions in all areas of life. Why go to a grocery store to shop when you could order food to be delivered? Why go to the library, when everything was on the internet anyway? Frisk painted a utopian picture where we could control our daily lives from the home, isolated from the outside world but always connected to a virtual world. I took in his vision of the future with affected enthusiasm, but inside I was screaming abuse at him.

What I really hate the most with doers is their optimism. Oh, how the world is full of opportunity, oh, what an exciting future! Do they not see that everything is emptiness, a chasing of the wind? Do they not hear that every ticking second means being one dig of the shovel closer to the grave and that mankind's pursuit of happiness always, without exception, leads to catastrophe? But they don't have time to listen, they're too busy building their Tower of Babel. I saw it in Frisk's eyes, they were alight with opportunities, limitless opportunities. It was no small source of entertainment for me, to think that he, in a world where everything is possible, where we can be whatever we want to be just by believing in it enough – professor, star in a musical, a woman – had chosen to be, yes, a salesman. He hadn't become an astronaut or solved the climate crisis. No. He sold things. And he saw it as an important mission, almost a calling. When he on one occasion quoted Confucius to illustrate his point, I couldn't help saying, with acted enthusiasm, 'Oh, so you have read the *Analects*?' I knew the answer, of course he hadn't read them, but I wanted to completely innocently put him in his place. The quote probably came from a book by some inspirational speaker, who in turn thought that by citing ancient wisdom they could brush over the fact that their philosophy was all smoke and mirrors. A bit of Plato here, a bit of Confucius there, taken from a book of quotes on the internet, because doers obviously do not read Plato, they don't have the time, no one does. No, give us the smartest things he said in a hundred and forty characters so we can wear his wisdom like an accessory for our own personal brand!

Frisk believed that there were great opportunities for me as a salesman, just so long as I was sufficiently 'hungry.' That was another real doer word. People clearly went round and were metaphorically hungry pretty much all over the place. Hungry for winning, for success – presumably a symptom of having never actually known real hunger. Just ambition. Desire. Greed. So, I showed off my absolute hungriest side, said that I had always set aggressive targets, always wanted to outdo myself, was never satisfied with mediocrity. I *deliver*, quite simply (oh, this sales talk) and am not satisfied, never relax, because you can always better yourself, always make progress, always hone your skills. And if I have occasionally not succeeded, then I have learnt from these mistakes and become even more *efficient*, even *sharper*, even *hungrier*. My metaphorical stomach was really rumbling. There was no mistaking my energy. I almost believed my own words. If I do say so myself, my acting was of the highest quality; Frisk nodded thoughtfully, almost moved, I thought. Maybe he recognised himself, as a young man, in me and felt touched, yes, that must have been it, as a doer is only moved by others if they are reminding him of himself.

In any case, I had him on the hook, he was listening attentively and asked several interested follow-up questions and for several minutes I had him spellbound. I laid it on thick, pretended that I had once sent completely the wrong products to a client but had succeeded in convincing them that they were just what they needed, instead of the original order. 'You don't want grey chairs in your lobby, these red leather sofas are so on trend. And the comfort!'

I was like a fisherman straining the truth. A two kilo pike became a ten kilo pike, no, a ten kilo perch. From the quay. With an ordinary rod. I enjoyed the situation a bit too much and had to restrain myself from climbing down from the quay and, so to speak, walking on water. Frisk swallowed every word though, as doers are often gullible, in spite of being so false themselves and they really ought to be able to recognise a lie when they hear one. But no. In his eyes I was a great doer.

The job would include a lot of travel, he said, was that a concern for me? No. I loved being out on the road, to be constantly in motion. Was that not in fact what life itself was all about, moving forward? He smiled. But why this job specifically, why had I applied here? Was it the products that were interesting? I of course could not tell him the truth. I had actually applied for just one sales job to complete my little research project (a salesperson would naturally have applied for more), but that I chose precisely this one was more to be considered as chance, it was the first job in sales that turned up. I couldn't say that. There had to be something special with this company, what could it be? Yes! There was something about how they kept up with current trends, always seemed to have their finger on the pulse, to feel when the next change in beat was coming. They adapted to the times and did not get stuck in old habits. I saw that Frisk was flattered, it was probably due to his clarity of vision that the company could be considered in that light. Flattery always works on doers, they shamelessly receive compliments as if they were children. The doer has all of the child's undesirable qualities – selfishness, ignorance, greed – without showing signs of any of the accompanying redeeming aspects.

The Soulless continued with his questions. Where did I see myself in the future? In exactly the same place as now, my internal voice answered. At home, unmoveable, the same as I have always been. Be. Don't do, do, do. My outer voice said something completely different. I wanted to earn money, I said, but that was not the most important thing, I wanted to make an impression. If I got the chance, precisely this company would probably still be the arena for my *tour de force* for ten, twenty years. No, of course I didn't use the expression *tour de force*, this was after all a salesperson I was talking to.

I hit the jackpot with every answer, I could feel it, he hadn't said it yet, but the look on his face made it clear that the job was mine. He passed his hand through his hair, that heavily pomaded hair, and we were quiet for a moment. Every pause was filled with a low chattering from a commercial radio station playing on the doer's computer, banterous voices laughed and joked irrepressibly from the speakers as if everything was fine. It made me think of the *Titanic's* violinists. The vessel starts taking in water, but they play on. No one is suspicious or asks questions, we have built an unsinkable ship, an unsinkable Sweden, so we laugh falsely and talk over each other so that nobody notices that we're bound for hell. The radio voices joked about trivialities, something that happened in the toilets, haha. Traffic jams, haha, a text message that was sent to the wrong person, haha.

A person's choice of radio station reflects who they are. Frisk's personality was no more than a mashup of borrowed wind from other superficial individuals. It is ironic that this evil species has never met with their own dark side, never confronted it and doubted themselves. They do not know themselves. If they did, they would not just doubt, they would despair. If they could see their own perniciousness, experience the withering shame that knowing yourself and your own inadequacy implied, the doer would cease doing, the salesperson would cease selling! But I kept on Frisk's side, I was there as an ally, I came with peaceful intentions. The most noble would have been to awaken him from his secure slumber, to actually destroy his illusions. It is after all the truth which sets us free. But, I thought, my vocation was even higher: to study doers at close quarters and to present my scientific findings to the world.

Frisk could easily be fifty or so, but with the eternally youthful appearance that characterises his type, those who do not experience the same weight of gravity as the rest of us. He was blond too, which further emphasised his youthfulness. There is something insidious about grown men who are still bright blond. I don't trust them. Smooth cheeks, non-existent eyebrows. There was something unhealthy in this boyishness, it was as if he was stubbornly hanging onto his childhood. Adult, blond men are their own race, I thought as we sat there, a mythological and ill-natured race. But I smiled my most friendly salesman smile to this goblin and asked interesting questions to better understand the job. It was just a matter of formalities now, I could feel it, he could just as well finish up and say see you on Monday, there's your office, we'll organise a company car.

Instead, we slid into small talk, which is every doer's and salesperson's forte. Renovations, cars, sport. All the frivolities which are the badges of a soulless life. I felt helpless, blindsided. The bastard! I had carefully prepared for the role of aspiring salesperson, I had learned their vocabulary and imposing manner, but had completely missed this elementary weapon in every truly vapid individual's armoury. Small talk was such a given that I hadn't spared it a thought! I started to sweat and felt my confidence leaving me. I became a nodding, smiling, goofy, blushing, nervous schoolboy. He'd bought a boat, ok, what do you ask someone about that? All I could do was nod wide-eyed and whistle to demonstrate my reverence. He kept my eye as if waiting for a verbal reaction. I carried on nodding to show how impressed I was, but could not get any words out. Not after five seconds, nor after ten. He was torturing me! It was a battle which played out between us and he was the alpha male. He had hustled me into the corner of the ring, was jabbing frenetically and I hung on the ropes, punch-drunk and powerless.

Finally I succeeded in forcing out a question. 'Driving license,' I gasped. 'What's the deal with driving licences, do you have to have one? For the boat, I mean,' I said.

The look he gave me then made me realise that my research project had failed. It was as if he realised in exactly that moment that I was a completely different creature to himself and his smile was of a new kind. At first confused, then merciful – or acted merciful, as mercy does not exist with doers – in any case it was a smile directed at the idle loser, Fredrik Jansson.

We both sat in silence for a long time. The enchantment under which I had been holding him was now broken. He could see again, the veil had fallen from his eyes. Woken from his hypnosis, he now saw me for who I really was: a person who deeply disdained him. I knew nothing about boats, I didn't care. I knew nothing about the world in which he moved. I gave up the pretence. My posture regained its careless shape, my eyes shrank, my jaw muscles tightened. I smiled at him and for the first time my smile gave away my true feelings for him. He looked suddenly uncertain, almost afraid. I wanted to ask him what he thought the point was, the point of his life, his little, pathetic life. I wanted to tell him that he had everything and yet nothing, that everything would be torn away from him sooner or later. Soon he would be lying dead in a bed or on a floor somewhere, cold and dead in a mortuary, dead and rotting in a grave. Dead, dead, dead. The seasons would pass without him, the world would continue to turn. People would laugh, he would be dead. People would work, drink coffee, take the bus, he would be dead. Some would maybe remember him for a while, then they too would die. The headstone would be there for a while longer, until he was just a name amongst thousands of other names of people who also died a long time ago. Then the grave would no longer be there, or even the graveyard where he lay. There would just be forest, or concrete. New generations, new ambitions, new vanities. A thousand years would pass, ten thousand years. His time here meant nothing, there wouldn't even be a trace of him anywhere. His life was just a brief parenthesis in an eternal nothingness. But for goodness' sake, drive your boat!

Then I heard his voice, as through a fog.

'What do you say about that?' he was saying.

'About what?' I said.

He laughed. 'I said that I would like you to start here as of October.'

'Start in October?'

'Yes.'

What came next happened in a trancelike state. I remember that I gratefully said yes to a salary, I don't know how much, we shook hands and I think that he showed me around. More handshakes, more salespeople, more grins and straight backs. He wanted me. It was incomprehensible. I hated him, he wanted me, he liked me. Ha! Me! I, who have never had a job. Oh, how naïve he was. Oh, what a useless people person!

I am going to have the chance to study them up close, I'll be able to practice their dark magic myself, spellbind innocent people with a smooth tongue, take their money in exchange for something they never knew they needed. But becoming like the doers, that will never happen. I am an infiltrator, nothing more.

Meanwhile, I'll be earning money. What do I care about money? And even if I were to use my money to create a little comfort, just the most ordinary things, that doesn't make me one of them. No, no, I'll just use their hospitality, just for a while, like a visitor to the country of mammon. Is it not in any case better that the money goes to me, who does not care about it, who has a healthy relationship with money, than that it goes to the doers? I know when enough is enough, I can set boundaries. Money doesn't mean anything to me, nor what it can buy. But if I do have money, then I may as well use it. For relaxation, for example. Scientific study is hard work, I'll need recuperation time. Of course studies are impacted by the environment in which they are carried out. I can create good conditions for further investigation by getting a more comfortable seat to sit on. An armchair would be practical, maybe some unassuming decoration as well, to rest the eyes on now and again. With simple means, I can make my academic project more efficient. All in the name of science!

I start tomorrow. I have already updated my wardrobe. Not because I want to follow their moronic trends, no, but if I am going to play a credible character, I need to create the right conditions. Shirt, tie. I look presentable, even stylish. That is completely unimportant to me, appearance is the last thing I care about, the absolute last thing. But as I don't care about how I look, it of course makes no difference if I look a bit more dapper, so long as it helps the cause. People notice me now, women say hello in a different way. Their gaze lingers a little longer. And they say beauty comes from within! Ha! I'm the same person, I'll never change. I'll just be using their own means against them.

That is why it's also important that I do a good job. The more I sell, the more money I make and in this way can continue to finance my project. I'll step into the doers' world to learn everything about them, how they think, where they get their motivation from. And finally, when I have gathered sufficient material, then I will present the results. It will be the most thoroughly executed psychological study ever carried out! Then the doer will be exposed, he will stand there naked and everyone will see him for who he is.

But until then, during a brief number of years, I will have to pretend to be one of them.

BIGGER THAN DYLAN

'Welcome, Irina,' said Bo Sundman.

That he had shaken her hand as if she was a completely normal applicant couldn't be held against him, thought Irina. How could he know that he was standing eye to eye with one of Sweden's great future artists? He would carry out the interview exactly as if she was just anybody, without blushing at all or feeling any form of deference. Maybe she would get the job, maybe not, but for him this would one day be a valuable memory. 'Like that time I interviewed Irina Pevitsa,' he would say and recall how that great artist at a historic moment applied for a job working for him as an assembler. That would be something for Gramps to tell the grandchildren. She allowed him that. Everyone needed to feel a little important now and then.

It was when she won a talent show at the City Hotel that she realised that it was singing she should be betting on. Some of the city's absolute best voices were there, so she was far from sure that she would take home the prize. But after a hard fought battle against especially one guy who did a solid Mavin Gaye impression, Irina succeeded in drawing the longest straw with her swinging version of 'I Will Survive.' It was a great day. Everyone around her said that she should apply for the TV program, *Pop Idol*. But why should she allow herself to be cast in such a fixed mould? She wanted to go her own way, tread musical paths that no one had previously wandered.

'Incredible that it's snowing already. It feels like we've just come back from the holidays,' said Sundman.

'Yes, it really does,' said Irina.

'Here. You have to have a hi-vis vest on in the factory.'

She put the vest on, Sundman opened a steel door and a metallic smell struck them. They went past a few men in earmuffs and a woman with a pallet jack.

Life could also be like this, Irina thought. Run the CNC machine, shrink-wrap pallets, live for the weekend; Friday beers, crisps and all that. And then clock in again. Monday morning, on with the steep toe caps. It was so good to know that she was just a visitor here and would never be anything other than that. Because this wasn't what she was supposed to do, not at all, she was destined for something bigger. But going to interviews had become a necessity for her; without them, she would not be paid her unemployment benefit. It was a moment of irritation, but definitely worth it. In principle, it was of course a good thing that the unemployed were forced to actively apply for jobs in order to receive their benefits. Otherwise people could stay at home lying on the sofa watching the shopping channel pretty much as they wanted and live off the effort of the employed. What sort of society would that lead to? No, work was a positive thing. They were good people, Sundman and his gang, they created gainful employment for the great masses. They were absolutely necessary, they played their part. Not everyone could be a creator or an artist, but everyone was needed. She had great respect for the ordinary people, it was after all for them that she created, to give them some breathing room in their arduous little existences. That Irina happened to collect benefits wasn't about exploiting the system, she was just buying herself some time. Time was necessary in order to create something exceptional and the job seeker's allowance just happened to be a means to have the space to realise her dreams. A bit like a student loan. She would pay it back ten, thirty, a hundred times over when she had her breakthrough.

She needed in other words to go regularly to interviews for jobs she didn't want. But she couldn't say that to Bo Sundman, the benefits people would quickly get wind of it. No, she had to make an impact that was just negative enough to scare him off from employing her, but sufficiently subtle that she wouldn't arouse suspicions as to her motives. She had to appear interested in the job but unsuited to it, a combination that she had become something of an expert of during the past year.

'I thought I'd tell you a bit about us while we walk and you can just stop me if you have any questions.'

'That sounds good,' said Irina.

'Then we can sit down afterwards and discuss in a bit more detail.'

'Yes, sir.'

'We have been around since 1982 and have had the same concept since. I say "we" but I first started here in

1990. That was when my brother and I took over. We do, you could say, everything within storage. Changing room lockers, as well as luggage lockers for train stations and other public spaces, all kinds of locker that needs to be more or less secure.'

'There you go,' said Irina.

'An average order is for around two hundred thousand kronor, which corresponds to about fifty lockers, depending on what kind it is.'

Irina had more important things to think about than Sundman's lockers. Like her upcoming studio recording time. She preferred to not compare herself with others, she had a unique sound, but if she absolutely had to draw some parallels then the music itself was a cross between Alanis Morissette and Sheryl Crow. Although her voice was more like Björk's, sort of elfin Nordic. That's what it would say in the reviews when her first record came out: 'Spellbinding Nordic debut.' Just a shame that people didn't buy records in the same way anymore. Her tracks could certainly be shared more quickly with digital technology, but it still felt special to handle a record sleeve, to leaf through the song lyrics. And it was the lyrics that were her strongest point. She'd written some really great songs. Mainly in English, it was after all the global language of music. Song lyrics came to her pretty much at any time. It usually started with an image, which laid the foundations for a story. They were songs that told stories that she wrote, almost in the country or folk tradition. Lyrically, she was most like Bob Dylan. But whereas he could be a little simplistic, she was always innovative. She had a deep source that poured out lyrics for her songs, things she had experienced and maybe her lyrics could be a support for those who had undergone similar experiences. Her life had hardly been a walk in the park.

Irina's thoughts were interrupted by Sundman's voice: 'We are seventy employees and have played at that level for around the last ten years. In on the right there is the coating machine. We stuck that in back in the nineties, we run uniquely with powder coating. We've chosen to do it in-house and it works well. Occasionally we take outside commissions for coating work to deliver a smooth finish.'

Irina nodded. 'Smooth finish. Got it.'

There are different ways of having an impact on the world. Politics was one of them. But music, it touched some deeper humanity. And anyway, music opened doors to politics. Just look at Bono, who was received by presidents and popes. But in spite of all of Irina's intelligent thoughts about politics, she was an artist not a politician. An artist who defended freedom, justice and peace, yes, but an artist all the same. It was art which had the ability to reach deep inside, it was art which got the whole of society to change. The Berlin Wall, it didn't fall from Ronald Reagan's shouting and pleading, no, it was only after the singer David Hasselhoff took the mic that East and West Germany could be reunited. 'Looking for Freedom,' 'We Are the World,' 'Do They Know It's Christmas,' the list could go on – real change never comes from outside or from above, it comes from within, from the heart. No one could yet know what impact Irina's music would have on world history, but it would without any doubt make the world at least just a little bit brighter.

'And here we have the assembly. If you look up, you'll see our vacuum lift,' said Sundman and pointed at a device that was hanging down from the ceiling. It looked like a large hoover pipe with suckers on the end. 'That's to avoid heavy lifting. Lots of things are automated, but we'll never get by without human beings. Thank goodness, I should maybe add.'

'Yes, lucky,' said Irina.

They stopped at the assembly line. Another track came to her again. She heard the melody in her head.

A minor, C, G.

A minor, C, G.

Scuzzy guitars, a bit like Hendrix. No gimmicks, just rock, proper rock. Irina was swaying a little in time when a woman came up and stood by what was clearly her spot on the assembly line.

'Hey there!' the woman said. She looked at least fifty, had highlights in her hair and a chiselled, almost manly face.

'This is Agneta,' said Sundman. 'She has been with us longer than anyone. When was it you started? Eighty-eight?'

'Eighty-six,' said Agneta and looked at Irina. 'The idea was that I would just stay here for a year.'

When she smiled Irina saw that she was missing a tooth from her lower jaw.

'Not everyone knows this, but Agneta had a completely different career back then,' said Sundman. 'Tell Irina.'

'Oh,' laughed Agneta. 'Don't remind me about the indiscretions of my youth.'

Sundman turned to Irina. 'Agneta was close to making the big time in the eighties,' he said.

'The big time?' said Irina.

'I had naïve dreams back then.'

'Don't be so shy,' said Sundman. 'Stikkan Anderson wanted you! You were compared with Joplin.'

'Yes, yes,' said Agneta. 'Nothing came of it. And just as well, because I'm happy where I am.'

'What happened?' said Irina.

'Oh, what happened? Life! Life happened, Irina!' Agneta looked directly at Irina. 'Life happens to all of us. Sooner or later. Thirty years, it goes by in a moment, I'm telling you. I still feel like I'm twenty-five.'

She laughed and coughed, marked by the solariums and cigarettes. What a waste, thought Irina and felt a vague feeling of disgust which she quickly supressed.

'Agneta is the one who has a handle on this place. What she doesn't know, isn't worth knowing,' said Sundman.

'If you say so,' said Agneta and cough-laughed again.

Irina and Sundman walked on, through a door and into a large open space where a number of pallets lay ready, loaded with large boxes.

'That's where the goods go out,' he said and pointed towards a warehouse door. He looked at his watch. 'It's usually completely full here by three o'clock.'

'Yes.'

Irina felt how some lines of lyrics were beginning to take form:

Standing on the concrete floor. Going through the magic door.

Could there be something there? Slightly mystical. What is this door and why is it magic? And how can you *stand* on a floor and at the same time *go* through a door, was that not a contradiction? It was an opening line that definitely left you wanting more. That was her signature, starting with something cryptic or paradoxical, only to then tie it all together with a thread that cast light over the whole song. She was a master at it, allowing the listener to hang loose, invent their own associations. In everyone's life there are floors, in everyone's life there are doors, some of them are magic.

They went round the whole factory, Irina got to try some lockers, they went past Agneta again who waved and then they went into the office area. Sundman opened the door to his own office and let Irina go in first.

'What a nice setup,' Irina said and looked around. She now had to up the acting a notch. She shouldn't need to hang around here too long. She pointed at a photograph of a woman which stood on the desk. 'Is this your mum?'

'That's my wife,' said Sundman.

'Oh right. Nice.'

'Thank you. Take a seat here.'

They sat down.

'Some people just look older, that's how it is,' said Irina.

'Yes, we all age at a different speed,' Sundman said calmly and picked up a notepad that he had in his lap.

'But she doesn't have an illness or anything, that makes her age extra quickly? I saw a documentary where there are some people who age, like, five times faster than others. There's nothing up like that?'

'No, she's pretty sprightly, I have to say. But thank you for your concern.'

He was unbearably calm, thought Irina and answered her questions with genuine warmth.

'Why have you applied for this job?' asked Sundman.

'I was fired from my last job and need a new one. And this seems interesting, like.'

'And that was three years ago?'

'That I got fired? Sounds about right.'

Standing on the concrete floor, going through the magic door. I'm not a bore, I want to soar.

Now things were happening, Irina felt it. English was almost as natural to her as Swedish. Or even more natural, it just rolled off the tongue better, *for fuck's sake. Damn*, right? There were certain things you just couldn't express in Swedish, *shit*, like.

'We are very quality orientated here,' said Sundman. 'What is quality focus for you?'

'Let's see now. Quality. Which one is that again? There's quality and then there's what's it called? Quantity?'

'Yes.'

'Which is which? I always get them mixed up,' said Irina.

'Quality is if something is good or not. Quantity is to do with amounts,' said Sundman.

'Exactly, yes. Yep, that one then!'

'Which one?'

'What you said. That quality is if something is good or not. So that's what quality focus is then, I reckon. When it's simply good, focus on that. Quality focus, focus on quality.'

'Ok,' said Sundman. He wrote on the notepad. 'What are your ambitions for the future?'

'Are you writing down what I'm saying?' asked Irina.

'Yes, here and there.'

'So smart. So that you'll remember, right?'

'Exactly.'

'Awesome. Right, my ambitions…' said Irina. She squinted, grabbed the bridge of her nose between thumb and forefinger. 'Sorry. I'm just so hungover. Say it again, I'm listening now.' She looked up at him.

'Well, I was wondering what your ambitions are,' said Sundman.

'Ambitions, that's it, yes,' said Irina. 'My head is just pounding.' She closed her eyes and held up a hand as if to stop him from disturbing her, as if the slightest breeze would make her puke. She breathed in through her nose, out through her mouth. 'Wait.'

'Was it a big night?' asked Sundman carefully, without any sign of reproach in his voice.

Irina nodded, still with her eyes closed. 'Quite, yes. It was my birthday.' In through the nose, out through the mouth.

'Oh, congrats! Was it a big party then?'

'No, just me.'

Sundman nodded. 'Are you ok to continue?'

'Yep. It usually goes away quite quickly, it just comes on suddenly sometimes.'

'I know that it can be tough,' said Sundman. 'Take the time you need.'

Irina took the time she needed. A minute or so. A minute of controlled breathing in and out with closed eyes. Sundman didn't seem to be in a hurry, he sat calmly and watched. He was disturbingly patient.

'Now,' she said at last. 'Right, you asked about ambitions. I was thinking about being the boss in the long term.'

'Oh yes, the boss? That's a good goal to have. I should say that there are good career possibilities here. What would you say is good leadership?'

Irina stretched, ostensibly no longer hungover. 'If I can put it like this… I have younger siblings and that has made me a natural leader. I know how to bring people into line. If you've shown them who's in charge early on then you avoid any problems with recalcitrance later on. Once bitten, twice shy, that's my motto.'

'You mean that it's important to create clear boundaries?'

'Clear boundaries, yes, that's an important part of it. But it's about always handing out the right dose of punishment.'

'What are your thoughts on that?'

'It's no astrophysics. Pavlov already showed that it's just a matter of conditioning.'

'The thing with the dogs?'

'Yes, exactly. And we are basically animals. But it isn't just punishment that is important, you need to reward as well. 'Good job, you can have another biscuit, clever pooch.' Encourage good behaviour, punish bad. Immediately. Cows don't go near the electrified fence you know, they have learned not to. But the punishment has to come straight away so that they really connect their actions with it. That's how they learn.'

Sundman wrote something down. 'So why do you want to be the boss?'

'As I said, I'm a natural leader. People do what I tell them to.'

'They do what you tell them to?'

'They do what I tell them. When I use my harsh voice, everybody does what I tell them to.'

'Is that leadership for you? Being obeyed?' Sundman clearly wouldn't let himself be provoked. Every question was asked with a genuine tone of interest.

'No, of course not just that. The main thing is getting people to do what you want, but at the same time getting them to believe that it's also what they want. Maybe even getting them to think that they were the ones taking the initiative in the first place. That requires a slightly deeper psychology,' she said and made it sound like it was a little above his level.

'Can you give an example?'

Irina thought. The new track was still pumping away somewhere in the back of her head, it would be called 'Concrete Floor' and that was what she really wanted to be focused on but she needed to be present in the interview. And this Sundman was sly, he didn't seem to put much weight on the fact that she was clearly pathological in some way. Instead of provoking him, she felt herself provoked, by his calmness.

'An example,' repeated Sundman. 'Give an example of how you can help employees to feel a part of things.'

'Well, so long as you're the boss, you can come up with your own methods,' said Irina.

Sundman laughed. 'That's true. I also wanted to ask you, as you are such a natural leader, how your relationships are with your own managers? Do you manage to follow orders?'

'So what, you don't think I'd be able to do that?'

'I'm just asking.'

'Yeah, and I'm wondering why you are asking. Do you think that I seem like someone who can't follow orders? Is that what you think? Do you seriously think that I'm some sort of idiot?'

Irina felt a little bad for Sundman. He was so kind that it pinched at her to be so mean, but she was obliged to get him to doubt in her abilities. She knew exactly when that moment came in an interview, the moment when the interviewer completely lost interest in her. She had been there many times. Sometimes it happened after a couple of minutes, sometimes after ten. But she had still not reached that level with Sundman. It wasn't personal, but she was forced to be irritating.

'I am sure that you are capable of following orders,' said Sundman. 'Let me ask this then: what are your expectations of this role?'

Irina gave him a look as if she was reluctantly accepting his words as an apology. She sighed.

'I expect the work to feel meaningful.'

Sundman brightened up. 'You really mean that, don't you?'

'Really mean what?'

'When you say that you want the job to feel meaningful, that's the real Irina Pevitsa talking, right? I thought that it was hilarious when you were joking, but it's interesting to hear you being serious too.'

'Joking? About what?'

'Haha! The thing about punishing employees, I thought that was funny. Irony. Totally my kind of humour. We could have a lot of fun working together here. And I absolutely believe that you will think that it's meaningful.'

'You're making a mistake! I wasn't joking. This is how I am. Authoritarian, megalomaniacal. That's me in a nutshell.'

'You really are funny!' said Sundman. 'You can go far with humour. I'm convinced that you'll do damn well here.'

'Thanks.'

Irina was sweating. What was the guy talking about? His kindness was close to choking her, she couldn't puncture his inflated optimism. Was she about to lose control of this situation? If she was offered the job, she would be forced to accept. No more benefits, no more time for creating. That couldn't happen.

'What are you interested in learning?' asked Sundman.

There was a knock at the door. It was Agneta.

'Hey!' she whispered carefully. 'I just wanted to let you know I'm off now.'

'That's fine, Agneta. You don't need to tell me, you know that I trust you.'

'I still wanted to.'

'I appreciate it.'

Agneta smiled to Irina and gave her a thumbs up. 'Good luck,' she whispered and closed the door.

Irina's heart was beating out of her chest. Agneta's face, her toothless smile, it disturbed her so much. Once upon a time, she too had been promising, but life had happened. Life. Irina didn't want it. Life, that was no life at all. Being offered the job just wasn't an option. Was she going to be here in thirty years, toothless and dreamless, telling new staff about how she once almost wrote a hit single, how she was almost world famous, how Bob Dylan almost called her up to say thanks, how she almost… No. She would find a way of getting Sundman to cross her off his list.

'Guess what?' she said. 'I can stand on my hands. I'll show you!'

'You really don't have to,' said Sundman.

Irina had already got up. 'Yes, it's no problem, check this out.'

She checked that the floor in front of her was clear. Took a deep breath, bent over forwards and spread her palms out on the floor, at the same time as she lifted one leg kind of backwards and upwards. With a grunt she got the other foot off the floor but immediately fell forwards with a thud.

'Damn it. It normally works. I just need to relax for a moment. Give me a second.'

'I believe you, sit down again and we can talk about salaries.'

Salary? Irina was terrified. This could mean the end for her as an artist, before she had even begun. Earmuffs, work gloves, disillusionment at an assembly line. No! In a moment of pure panic she thought that a failed cartwheel might make him change his mind.

'Check this out first,' Irina said.

She blew on the palms of her hands, clapped them hard and rubbed them together. Then she slapped her thighs, like a high jumper. A few deep breaths. Focus. 'Come on now,' she said quietly, as if she was trying to beat her own personal best. She then stretched her arms up and let her whole body fall hands first towards the floor.

Then it went black.

A sharp pain in the leg was the last thing she remembered when she woke up. She hurt all over, but especially in the knee. Two paramedics stood bent over her.

'She's woken up,' said one of them.

'Good morning,' said the other one and smiled to Irina.

'What happened?' she asked.

'You've dislocated your kneecap. It's not serious, but we'll take you with us so we can get a look at your head to make sure you aren't concussed.'

'She's focusing well, she just seems to have fainted. That can happen with the pain. Irina, can you hear me ok?'

Irina nodded.

Sundman stood with his hands in his pockets and looked at her. He looked ashamed.

'There was a proper crack. I should really have pushed the chairs in before you cartwheeled. I'm sorry. We need to think more about health and safety here. I'll deal with it. We'll of course do everything we can do compensate you for this.'

'No problem,' said Irina.

The paramedic had rolled a gurney in.

'We'll lift you up now, ok? One, two, three!'

Sundman walked next to the gurney as Irina was wheeled out.

'I'll call and see how you are doing, so you can start here in your own time. They think you should be able to get going already in a week.'

SLOW COOKER SATURDAYS

It was an advert in the local paper which got my interest, a small box with a mobile number. "Translator needed. French to Swedish." So I called Renate Schmidt. She ran a small translation agency and had recently received requests for translations from French, a language she didn't yet cover in-house, she explained. It wasn't a full-time position, of course, it would lead to the odd commission now and then and I needed more to do.

We agreed to meet at a café. I got there first and took a seat furthest in with my back to the wall, to have a view of the room. That was the place where I always sat, it was in many ways my local, this café, I went there at least once a week. I had seen a picture of Schmidt and kept an eye out for someone who looked like her. The problem was that she looked a bit non-descript in the photo. There were a couple of times that I was unsure, when customers came in. Could that be her? Or her? I tried to make eye contact, but could tell from the women's determined gaze at the pastries that none of them were Schmidt. When she did then tumble in the door in the flesh, I was so undoubtedly convinced that it was her that I wondered how I could have confused her with those other women. The bell over the door rang wildly and she slipped, covered in fresh snow which she laughingly shook off herself, quickly apologising to the passing waitress. She brightened up when she saw me as if she recognised me too, waved and mouthed a 'hi' before she zigzagged over to my table.

'Have you already ordered? Or what would you like?' she asked and pointed with her thumb over her shoulder.

'Just coffee, I was thinking. With milk. But I can…'

'I'll do this,' she said and motioned to me to stay seated.

She came back with a cup of filter coffee for each of us, hers black and mine white. A pastry, hers I guessed, was on a white plate between us. I sipped the coffee. She moved the pastry towards her and broke it into two parts. She stuck one half in her mouth and held the remaining half in a firm grip in her other hand.

'I'm so hungry,' she said. 'Just come from the gym, the new one, have you been there?'

'No, I haven't,' I said.

'You have to go. If you do, then you have to try BB.'

'BB?'

'Body Balance.'

'Right, is it good?'

'It wipes you out. Like, *completely* wipes you out. What workouts do you normally do?' The pastry muted all her consonants.

'Nothing really. I go for a walk now and then,' I said.

Schmidt smiled, as if I had made a joke. The question is never *if* you work out, it's always *what*. What workouts do you do? She gave me a few more seconds to clarify that I was joking – that was what her blinking expression meant – but I didn't take the opportunity, I didn't have anything to add. She gave up and looked down at the empty plate.

'Oh I could eat another one. No, that's enough.'

She pushed the plate away from her, stood up and hung her coat on the chair back. Her blood sugar level had clearly recovered.

'Great that you could come, Camilla. I've looked through your work samples. They look good.'

'Thank you,' I answered. 'I have more in case you need them.'

Schmidt wasn't listening, she seemed pre-occupied with something that was happening at another table. She leant forwards and whispered.

'Did you see that artist? No, don't look now. On your right, by the window. Turn round slowly.'

I turned around. There was a young guy in a beret. He was drinking coffee and reading a paperback. Now and then he looked out of the window. Schmidt carried on whispering:

'I mean, what on earth? A beret? Talk about crying out for attention.'

She sniggered mischievously. I smiled.

'I thought it was kind of stylish,' I said.

'Oh,' she said and fanned her face with her hand, 'now I'm getting the sweats. Phew!'

'Oh dear.' I tried to summon some form of interest in my voice.

'Have you been here before?' she asked.

'Yes, I come here from time to time actually. I like this place. Unassuming, somehow.'

'It's nice, isn't it?' She looked at the empty plate sadly, as if the now eaten pastry symbolised the transience of everything, as if she was thinking that all which is good must, sooner or later, come to an end. Life, pastries. But then a new thought seemed to give her expression its light back.

'So, do you have children?'

'No, no children.'

'Husband? Boyfriend?'

'Yes. Well… he died,' I said. 'It was three years ago.'

'Oh dear.' She looked away, back at the artist, held her mug to her mouth. Slurped meditatively.

'Oh dear,' she repeated.

I don't know what I had expected. Maybe a 'sorry' or 'that's terrible to hear.' But nothing like that. No follow-up questions either. Just a blank stare out into the ether. Not that I wanted to discuss the subject further. On the contrary, the boyfriend question was the one I was absolutely the least keen to answer, as my answer always led to a serious conversation with people I didn't want to have serious conversations with. Oh, how horrible, oh, poor me and so on. But Schmidt's reaction was worrying for the opposite reason; she was almost eerily apathetic.

'Cancer,' I said. A little brashly, I must admit, to make her uncomfortable, to test her.

'Uh-huh.' She nodded. It was the kind of nod of the head you get when you say that you live in the suburbs, or that you've started playing golf. 'Uh-huh, yep. I see.' Then she broke into a big smile.

'Well, I've got two kids, it's hard work, you know. Girls. Four and two.'

'I understand,' I said.

'Here!' she said and opened her purse out on the table and pointed. 'Alice. She's the lively one. Full speed ahead. And Siri. She just smiles. Loves cookies. "Cookies," she shouts, "cooookies!"'

The pictures had place of honour in her purse, inside a see-through pocket. Schmidt laughed and shook her head. She still held her purse under my nose. I nodded and smiled. She still held it there.

'Lovely. Must be fantastic,' I said.

'Fantastic? You said it. Fantastic is what it is. That's life, Camilla. Life. We have to find someone for you too!'

'It's not my top priority right now,' I said.

She folded her purse away and leaned forward. Tenderly, slowly, with a serious expression.

'I'm worried about you Milla. Of course you have to meet someone. Live a little. Fall in love. You can't go around dwelling on the past.'

Milla. Nobody, as far as I could remember, had ever called me that before.

'You don't need to worry,' I said. 'I like being on my own. At least for now. It wasn't something I wished for, being alone. But someone new... it isn't particularly urgent. It's been a while since he died, but still. I talk to him occasionally, you know, about everyday things.'

'Whoo, spooky,' she said and shook her hands in front of me. She laughed.

'Yes, no, not like that,' I said. 'I'm not holding séances or anything.'

She continued to laugh, now even louder. Something about the word séance was clearly hysterically amusing.

'You are too fun, Milla. Séances! I'm dying! More coffee?'

She sprung up and snatched our mugs away with her. A chance to change subject, I hoped. I just wanted to cut to the chase, talk about the translation work, the salary. She came back and theatrically handed me my mug, in the manner of an obsequious servant and exclaimed:

'Pour madame!'

She sat down. 'Yep, French then,' she said. 'Are you quick?'

'At translating?'

'Yes. How long does a page take?'

'Oh, well it really depends on what the text is. And how much text is on the page and so on. But if I was translating a tourist brochure then I'd maybe manage five hundred words an hour.'

'Sounds good,' said Schmidt absently. She leaned her head on one side, it seemed as if she did it every time she came to think of her children, and smiled a little.

'So, yesterday I had to go several rounds with Alice when it was her bedtime. I was forced to wrestle her to the floor in the end.'

I thought that Schmidt would be a tough opponent in a wrestling match. Slippery somehow, you'd never be able to get hold of her. Low centre of gravity. I imagined us in a wrestling ring, her in blue and I in red. She was rounded, but in a fit sense. I guessed that if she took off her clothes, everything would be in the right place. No wobbling, no hanging. She had a firm body, quite simply, gym-solid. No visible fat but no visible muscles either, just an indefinable mass fixed in a tight skin. High density. Her face was narrow. She was beautiful, beautiful but deadly on the wrestling mat, that was clear. I was glad that I would probably never need to feel her strength, her meaty chest in my face, crushed by her unbendable will and equally unbendable arms.

'I understand that it can be tough,' I said, still with an image of myself being choked in her cleavage.

'What's that?' she said.

'Children.'

'Ah, they're wonderful, absolutely wonderful. Yesterday they did drawings for daddy. Siri just doodles, but Alice, well, it was really impressive. She's only four, but paints like a six year-old.'

She buried her fingers in her handbag. 'Wonder if I didn't bring a drawing with me. No, it must still be at home. Yep, yes.'

'That's a shame,' I said, but felt relieved to not have to pretend to be impressed by some children's drawings that doubtless looked like any other children's drawings. Even though Schmidt's kids were of course *really* special, not at all like every other child whose parents think that their child is special. That was certainly how it was, I thought, her children were certainly geniuses, they were presumably the renaissance personified.

Unlike children themselves – who, at a certain age, realise that their parents are not superheroes – parents never stop believing that their children are extraordinary. It's a lifelong delusion. Some manage to keep it a secret, but all parents genuinely believe that they have given birth to da Vinci. Schmidt was visibly convinced of it and not ashamed of the fact.

'Let me see if I have any pictures on my phone,' she said and took her phone out.

She refused to give up. I leant politely over the table to see as she quickly swiped through picture after picture. I caught glimpses of cocktails with sparklers, suntanned faces, feet pointing at an ocean horizon, feet on a sandy beach, footsteps in the sand, sunsets, mountaintops reflected in ski goggles, victory signs and losers' pouts, children in a pool, children with superhero outfits, children on tricycles, more children, perhaps the neighbours' children.

'Here,' she said at last and turned the mobile towards me.

It was a stickman, drawn by a kid who halfway through seemed to have thought 'oh, bollocks to it' and scribbled over everything with a red crayon.

'Wow!' I said. 'Did you say she was four? Just four?'

'Isn't it incredible?'

'Yes, incredible,' I said.

Schmidt lapped up the praise. She turned the phone back towards herself and admired the drawing. For quite a while in fact. She emitted small, cute sighs.

'What kind of commissions do you mainly need help with?' I asked, when I decided that she was ready.

She cleared her throat. 'You'll see that there's someone out there for you too. So that you can experience this,' she said.

'Yes. I'm sure there is,' I said. 'So, I was just wondering what kind of translations were involved?'

'It's mainly… brochures. Instruction manuals and such.' She started playing with her hair.

'Are there lots of technical descriptions then?' I asked.

'Look!' said Schmidt and tapped me on the hand. 'He's got a pocket watch. He can't be serious.' She was looking over at the artist again.

I decided to not turn around. 'Well, there you go,' I said.

'I've been wondering whether I should let Alice start going to dance lessons. I think it's a good idea that she does some activities. Anyway. Enough babbling about my children,' she said and smiled apologetically. Judging by her expression and tone however, she was full of conviction that her children genuinely, completely objectively, were one of the most interesting subjects for conversation two people could find and that Alice and Siri formed a basis for discussion that was every bit as inexhaustible as the theodicy dilemma or the meaning of life. That someone could honestly show a lack of interest in the subject was no doubt a thought that had never crossed her mind and so her apology was a formal courtesy, to which I was expected to respond with the words 'no, you're not babbling at all, it's fascinating.' And so I did.

'No, you're not babbling at all, it's fascinating.'

'Do you think so?' she asked.

'Yes, really.' I couldn't look her in the eye.

'Because it *is* a balancing act,' she said. 'You want to encourage your children, but not to stress them out. Give them the opportunity to develop.'

'Yes, I can imagine…'

'I can hardly remember what it was like before I had children. What is it actually like to be childless? What do you do with all the time you have?'

'I don't know, I don't have anything to compare it with…'

'Don't tell me! You crochet or knit, right?'

'I do actually, occasionally. Crochet.'

Schmidt clapped her hands with excessive enthusiasm. 'I knew it! Jumpers? Hats?'

'Well, a bit of everything,' I said and tried to get back to talking about the job.

'What is the extent of it?'

'What's that, how do you mean?'

'The job.'

'Ah yes,' Schmidt said and ran her finger along the rim of her coffee cup, as if to try and get a musical note out of it.

'It's quite variable, it can change from month to month. But you are interested?'

'I am, but I'm anxious that it may not be consistent enough that I would be able to rely on an income.'

'About that!' said Schmidt and suddenly slapped both her knees in a rocking chair motion. 'I met a girl the other week who insisted that she earned at least forty thousand kronor a month. Do you know what she does?'

'No.'

'She sells adverts. On the internet. Quite incredible!'

'Yes.'

'I think that the internet is the future.' She said it as if she was sitting on something explosive. She lowered her voice. 'Everything is on the internet. Everything.'

It was as if she wanted me to remember where was when I first heard it. 'The internet is the future.' I wanted to scream.

'How many hours do you think it would involve per month? Roughly?' I asked carefully.

She smiled fawningly and almost sweetly.

'You're funny! I recognise myself in you. We're the type that wants to be in control, right? I've really had to teach myself to chill out a bit, you can't control everything. If there is one thing this life has taught me, it's that there is no instruction manual, not even if you're a translator. Relax Milla, it'll be fine!' She took hold of my hand.

I smiled. 'You're right,' I said. I couldn't disagree, I couldn't. And I couldn't pull my hand away either.

'You and I, we are twin souls. I can feel it strongly. Just now, in here.' Schmidt beat twice on her own chest.

I scratched my face. 'Right, wow.'

She broke into a big smile. 'You feel it too? I can see it on you!'

I tipped my head as if to neither say yes or no. But my confirmatory smile was grist to her mill.

'Twin souls!' said Schmidt. 'Right? We think the same. I remember what it was like. I've been to interviews as well. The uncertainty, but at the same time the ambition. That inner voice that says "Go for it." Go, go, go. Out into the unknown.'

'Exactly,' I said.

I wanted to get away from this discussion about twin souls but my politeness stopped me from putting up a fight. 'Go for it, just go,' I echoed and hated myself for it.

She looked at my coffee mug. 'I know what you're thinking. "Will she suggest another refill?" That's *exactly* what I'm going to do! Coffee with milk, Milla always has milk in her coffee,' she said and winked at me. She took both mugs with her to the counter. The artist was stood in the queue for coffee, Schmidt stood behind him. She looked at me, nodded discreetly at him behind his back. 'Beret,' she mimed and laughed silently with her mouth wide open.

I grinned back. She had turned this poor youth into a projection screen for our common humour. She and I, we now were twin souls. We were the kind of friends who could look at a person and both think the same thing, see the same hilarity in all of the everyday trivialities, where others didn't get it. It was true friendship, a shared view of the world, we danced completely in time with one another. Schmidt came back with the refilled mugs and sat down.

'I mean, your face when you saw that I was stuck behind that artist guy! I love your humour,' she said.

'The beret,' I laughed.

Why was I doing it? Why was I encouraging this lunacy? Why could I not just shake my head or ask her to cut it out? What was it within me that was seeking friendship with this person, what was it in my soul, that sought out its own downfall?

Schmidt simply enjoyed it, she understood that she had gained a new admirer. Now she could go full throttle. A kind of mischievous look crossed her face, the kind that only a girlfriend can have when they have something really funny to recount.

'A while ago I was asked if I had any German in me, as I'm called Schmidt,' she said. 'And I answered: "Sometimes I do. My husband is from Hamburg." Haha!' She laughed loudly. 'Get it? Any German in me! Like, a juicy bratwurst, right up in the bajingo!'

I didn't know where to look. It felt as if everyone's stares were drawn to her raucous laughter. Many of them must have heard her joke and, in their eyes, I was this vulgar woman's best friend, presumably just as debauched, if not worse. No! I don't know her, I wanted to shout, I came here for a job interview, I thought we were going to talk about translation work, I swear! I've never seen her before, this little powerhouse of a woman. Schmidt was sweating, fanning herself with her hand, the whole time just millimetres from a new laughing fit.

'How about, do you have any…' she started to shake, '…French in you?' She burst out laughing again.

I shook my head. 'No,' I whispered. 'Neither in the one sense nor the other.'

'That could be something?' She gave me a sort of forbidden look. 'An Alain or a François.' She stretched her hand out and mimed a clawing cat. 'Rooaar.'

I looked around. People seemed to be having their coffee in peace, no one was taking any notice of us. I breathed out.

'I have lived in France,' I said. It was an attempt to subtly move focus from her amorous insinuations to something that actually had relevance for the work in question.

'How romantic!' said Schmidt. She raised her eyebrows playfully: 'So maybe after all you have tried…'

'I studied there,' I interrupted, to avoid any further pronouncements on the intricacies of love-making. 'I read literature. It was tough at the start, with the language. Especially with all the nineteenth century authors. Hugo. Flaubert. It's hard enough in Swedish, with all the outdated vocabulary. But you get into it. Although the worst is probably still the twentieth century philosophers. They're incomprehensible, but for completely different reasons.'

Schmidt had picked up her mobile, looked at it distractedly, then looked round, stamped her feet on the floor. She sighed deeply and nodded.

'So!' she suddenly burst out. 'Speaking of books! Have you read *Fifty Shades of Grey*?'

'No, I haven't,' I answered curiously, as if I wanted to hear more.

'Do it!' She bit her bottom lip. 'Speaking of…'

I interrupted her again. 'I'll have to remember that one.'

I drank a little of my coffee, this had to be far too much by now, the third cup, but what could I do?

'But it's not a matter of literary translation in other words?' I continued. 'I've actually never worked with that, but at some point it would be exciting to have a go.'

'What were you saying? Work with what?' She fingered her phone again.

'With translation of literature.'

'Ah yes. No, no. Nothing like that,' she said mutedly and put her phone down on the table. She looked around the room, fiddled with her hair. She clearly swung between complete boredom and extreme enthusiasm. Which is to say, boredom when the subject was mine and enthusiasm when the initiative was on her side. She asked interested questions but when the answer came it was as if she turned off. We were twin souls, she had claimed, but I was obviously the little sister in some way, a little sister who was occasionally allowed to tag along with her older sister on her adventures, but a permanent number two at her side.

'Where do you live Milla?' she asked.

'I live in a flat a quarter of an hour from here.'

She nodded quickly. 'I live in a villa, in Bymarken. I don't think I could manage to go back to living in an apartment,' she said.

'It works well for me,' I said.

'Not being able to play music as loud as you want, no garden. Booking the laundry room. Who plans doing laundry a week in advance anyway? What kind of a life is that?' She shook her head. 'No, no. Villa life, that's what you need. You'll have to visit sometime, sample it.'

'Love to,' I said. Why, why?

'What are you doing on Saturday? I was thinking of using the slow cooker. What kind of wine do you drink?'

'Oh, right, Saturday?' I thought and thought. 'Let me see.' No, no, no, my mind had gone completely blank. Did I have a sister visiting? An ice-hockey game? Nothing seemed plausible, I couldn't lie. I *couldn't* lie, and felt myself dying inside. This was the end.

'I'm not doing anything special,' I whimpered.

'Favourite wine?'

'I've never really thought of it.'

'Something French, I'm thinking? Fruity?'

'Yes, that works.' Wine is just wine, I thought.

'I knew it. We have the same taste, you and I!' She got her mischievous look back. 'Get something French inside you.'

I smiled again. Oh, how I smiled, during the last hour I'd smiled more than I usually would in a week. So false, so hollow! Dinner, sure, would love to! A beret, haha! Please let me die before Saturday!

'Is it a big do?' I asked.

'We'll see. You're the first one I've invited. Worst case, it'll be just you and I sitting there, us bores, haha.'

I tried to laugh but ended up mainly just blowing air out my nose.

'That sounds fine,' I said.

I didn't care about the job, I just wanted to get out of this situation. Why was I always done in by this? I was a magnet for all these limited editions, random characters saw in me a potential BFF. All the meaningless social occasions I've had to suffer through, so many concerts and cinema trips and barbecue nights and Tupperware parties that I've put up with, just because I have never learned to say no. Maybe I could break my leg? Perhaps I didn't need to die to get out of it? Maybe just whack a sledgehammer into my shin, surely that would do it? 'I'm sorry, I was really looking forward to it but I've broken my leg.' That had to suffice?

I was seriously thinking all these thoughts, had started to wonder who would have a sledgehammer that they could lend me so I could get it done. It would hurt initially. Then a few weeks with a cast on, that wasn't a big deal? But she wouldn't give up because of one little broken leg, Schmidt, no, she would offer to pick me up, give me a lift in her car, make sure that I could stretch my leg out. Take care of her bestie. Give me a neck massage, maybe. She would enjoy it! And I would not be able to say no. It would have to be something worse, much worse.

I wondered for a while about the alternatives, when a towering man came into the café. He was walking over toward the till but stopped when he saw us, changed direction and came, smiling, right over to our table. Schmidt saw him out the corner of her eye, looked in another direction and covered half her face with her hand.

'Was it a cream bun today?' said the man, apparently directed at Schmidt. He stood a metre from our table, hung his scarf on the chair at the next table. He appeared to be about fifty, but something in his expression made me suspect that he was substantially younger. He had friendly eyes and a similarly friendly, greying beard. Schmidt didn't look in his direction. Instead she carried on talking to me:

'It'll be really fun. Then you'll be able to meet the children too. They will be so taken with you, I can just tell.' She spoke much more quietly now, and forcedly.

'Have you had any luck with a job yet then? Did anything happen with the Co-Op or what?' asked the man, while he hung up his coat with his back to us. Now he turned round and his and Schmidt's eyes met for the first time. She looked at him murderously.

He flung out his arms. 'I didn't mean to interrupt,' he laughed and walked off to order.

'What an idiot, that guy,' she said and followed him with her eyes. Then she looked at her watch.

'But wow, how time flies, now we have hardly had time to talk about the job.' She cast a glance at the till. 'But we

can discuss on Saturday, ok? Chez moi at seven o'clock.'
She got up quickly, hung her coat over her arm, grabbed her bag and strode over to the door. She turned and waved.

'Au revoir.'

INFECTIOUS LIKE EBOLA

A scent of soap and hand sanitiser struck Kent Eskilsson when he entered the room. It had been thoroughly cleaned, pedantically even, and was sparsely furnished. There were no textiles in the room, just steel and plastic, polished surfaces, strip lights which were reflected from all directions. White walls, white floor. It was a room designed to create headaches, it seemed, migraines and confusion. Inside the door was a container full of light blue shoe protectors, a pair of which he was clearly expected to put on. He stepped into the shoe covers, every movement he made gave an echo in the blank room. It felt like walking into the inside of a drum, thought Eskilsson. He reached out his hand to the man behind the desk, but he bowed in return instead. His figure was reflected in the highly polished surface of the desk. Eskilsson sat down on the visitors' seat on the other side of the desk.

'The role for which you are applying is haunted by bad luck. I want you to know that. Our first general secretary got aids, just like that. The one before him got meningitis and her predecessor was killed by a rare form of glaucoma. We've gone through seven general secretaries in four years. It is not good for the organisation,' the man said. He spoke as if the two of them had already warmed up, were through with the common courtesies and other small talk.

'That sounds terrible,' said Eskilsson.

'It's really just dumb luck that I'm still here as chairman after ten years. One never knows how long one will stay in good health.'

Åke Hanell, chairman of the board for the Royal Society of Hypochondriacs, took a pen out of the breast pocket on his short-sleeved shirt. Around his wrist was a bracelet in turquoise plastic, possibly a watch, it was hard to tell.

'Kent Eskilsson, wasn't it?' he said and made a note.

'Yes.'

Hanell looked up. 'And you have, as far as I can understand, never been ill?'

'Of course I've been sick, but very rarely. I'd say maybe four, five days' absence over the last fifteen years.'

In fact, these days were split across two occasions. In one case, Eskilsson's sick leave was due to an appendicitis, in the other it was food poisoning. Actually, that time, all his colleagues were ill too, some of them were off for a whole week. Eskilsson himself was back after a day in bed. Hanell seemed impressed.

'And no signs of illness recently?'

'No.'

Hanell stuck his pen subconsciously in his mouth, chewed gently on it before he realised his error and took it out again. He looked disgustedly at the pen, then at

Eskilsson, at the same time as he dropped the pen into a waste paper basket.

'There are both pros and cons to employing a hypochondriac for this role. The benefit is that the individual in question understands our fight, wants to take a part in it, is passionate about the job. The downside... well, as I said, seven general secretaries in four years. So we have thought about trying a different strategy. You seem, if I may say so, unashamedly chipper and carefree.'

Hanell opened a packet with a new pen, where the pen was encased in plastic like a toothbrush.

'I have never been one to worry about things too much,' said Eskilsson.

'But do you think that you could help our cause, even so?' Hanell threw the plastic in the bin and clicked the pen top twice, quickly.

'I think so, actually. I sit on the board for the Royal Swedish Society for the Deaf and I am not deaf.'

Hanell's eyes narrowed. 'Are you sure?'

'Haha, yes.'

'Some people are just really good at reading lips.'

'Yes.'

Hanell covered his mouth with his hand. 'Can you hear what I'm saying now?'

'I can hear you.'

Hanell took his hand away from his mouth. 'Ok, you aren't deaf. That must feel good? But you're still of help to the deaf, you think?'

'Yes, I believe so. I've been involved there for two years now.'

'Good. Good,' said Hanell. Then he sat in silence and thought for a moment, before he started to make gestures with his hands at the same time as he lip-synced. His lips made a moist, smacking noise.

'I don't know sign language,' said Eskilsson.

'Me neither. It would have been fun to know what that meant.'

'What what meant?'

'This,' said Hanell and threw his hands up again in wild movements. His face seemed to seriously mean what his hands were saying.

'Probably nothing,' said Eskilsson.

Hanell carried on for a moment, completely in character as a sign language interpreter. Eskilsson didn't move.

'Never mind,' said Hanell finally and stopped his performance. Instead, he picked up a brochure and handed it to Eskilsson. 'We work to draw attention to hypochondria in society. We write discussion pieces, we try to become more visible in different ways, to improve the everyday life of hypochondriacs. Make sure that resources are provided within society to make our lives more liveable. Above all, we want to get people to see hypochondria for what it really is, a sickness. It's our foremost goal, that hypochondria be recognised as a diagnosis by the National Board of Health and Welfare.'

Eskilsson flicked through the brochure. 'You mean that hypochondria is an illness?'

'Of course! It's incredibly limiting.' Hanell bristled indignantly. 'What would you call it yourself?'

'I thought that hypochondria was where you believe you have illnesses that you *don't* have.'

'Exactly, that is the illness.'

'But if you're actually ill, then you aren't hypochondriacs, as you're not imagining it.'

Hanell leaned forward. 'Wait a second there. We're not imagining that we are hypochondriacs.'

'No, I understand that,' said Eskilsson.

'We believe that we have *other* illnesses.'

'But how can you be sure that you are not imagining that you have hypochondria? If hypochondria is a real illness I mean, you said so yourself, then maybe you could just as easily be imagining that you are hypochondriacs. In the same way that you imagine you're diabetic or, I don't know, asthmatic.'

'You mean that maybe I'm not a hypochondriac at all?'

'I'm just playing with the idea. Maybe you're imagining it.'

'Yes, I imagine it. Hence I'm a hypochondriac.'

'Although you just said a minute ago that…'

Hanell made a stop sign with his hand. 'Enough about this, enough about this. All that's a bit convoluted for me. In any case, that's one aspect, pursuing the lobbying work. The other one, or the main one really, is taking care of our members. We want to give them useful information, spread knowledge about different types of affliction, what the signs are. Our newsletter is well read, I must confess. In the last edition we did a special on meningitis. It was lucky, I have to say, as that's how the previous general secretary spotted his symptoms.'

'Uh-huh.'

'Knowledge is the key here. We also normally run the most important headlines from other periodicals.' Hanell picked up a print-out of an article. 'Here, for example, from yesterday's newspaper: "Felt tired – had cancer." Or this one: "Thought it was a mosquito bite – died." It's important to keep up with the latest discoveries. Did you know that you can die from eating too much salt? And that you will definitely die if you don't eat any salt. It's about getting *exactly* the right amount. We are constantly balancing on a knife-edge. Death, life, death, life.' Hanell illustrated a set of scales which weighed life and death with his hands, they went up and down, back and forth.

'I've never thought about it in that way,' stated Eskilsson, in a tone that made it clear that neither would he ever think about it in that way.

'In practice, we are saving lives by keeping people updated,' said Hanell.

'Is there not a risk that you are fuelling your readers' concerns by enumerating all conceivable illnesses? It seems more likely to create hypochondria than to help people manage it. Surely what you want to do is to alleviate people's fears?'

Hanell smiled triumphantly, he seemed to have expected this outcome. 'The only way to really eliminate their concerns is to succeed in getting rid of…' He groaned and grimaced. 'Ow!'

'What?' said Eskilsson.

Hanell gritted his teeth and sucked air in between them. 'There's a pain in my scrotum. Do you get that sometimes?'

'I don't know. Is it like a stabbing pain?'

'No, more like a dull throbbing. Like it's vibrating a little.'

'Vibrating?'

'Yes. Zzzzz. That's what it sounds like. Zzzzzz.' Hanell raised his upper lip and shoved out his chin. 'Zzzzzz.'

'It's buzzing?'

'Yes.'

'Audibly, you mean?'

'I don't think so. Wait, now it's coming back, quiet. Listen. Come closer. No, not so close. There.'

Both of them sat there in silence, eyes turned upwards, focused. Eskilsson with his hands in his lap, Hanell with his forefinger in the air and hunched shoulders. Then he relaxed his shoulders and his finger.

'Now it's stopped,' said Hanell. 'Did you hear anything?'

'No. You?'

'No.'

'There's probably nothing to worry about, I wouldn't have thought,' said Eskilsson.

'Sure?'

'Fairly.'

'But not completely?'

Eskilsson considered this. 'You can never be completely sure.' Hanell began sweating profusely, drops ran from his hairline and down over his forehead, made their way past furrows and bumps in his skin and finally landed in his eyebrows, which became slick. He took a deep breath through the nose.

'That's exactly the problem. You can never be sure.'

He tore off a sheet of paper and wrote down a few words, out of sight for Eskilsson, threw his pen down and stuffed the piece of paper in his breast pocket, where there were already a number of notes. He picked up a tennis ball that was sat on the table and started kneading it with one hand.

'What would you be able to offer us?' he asked, but seemed to be somewhere else completely in spirit.

'Well, to start with, I've worked in healthcare for many years. Only in administration, technically speaking, but I am familiar with the environment. But above all I would be able to look at things in an objective light. I do understand that you are fighting a handicap the whole time and that you may need someone who sees a little more clearly.'

'Sees clearly, you say.' Hanell nodded. 'Clear sight is always needed. I would however point out that we see very clearly here, all us hypochondriacs. That may in fact be our principal characteristic. We see a little too clearly for our own good, we see risks to which others appear blind. You cough and you think, yep, that was just a cough. I cough and start to rattle off the ICD-10. No diagnosis is unknown to me. What is the cause of this cough? It could just as easily be COPD as dry air. It's about being prepared for the worst. I would say that there are probably no other people as well prepared as we are.'

'It sounds like you see your hypochondria as more of an asset than a handicap.'

'Yes and no, of course. All handicaps come with some benefit. In the way that you deaf people are really good at lipreading, for example.'

'I'm *not* deaf,' said Eskilsson, baffled and verging on annoyed.

'Oh no? But then how come you are so good at reading lips.'

'I'm not.'

'You said you were before,' said Hanell with a blank expression. He spoke with the nonchalance that belongs to only the supremely confident.

'No, I didn't, it was you who said that.'

Hanell chuckled superciliously. 'How could I know that you are good at lipreading if you hadn't said so yourself?'

'It doesn't matter. You were the one who said it,' said Eskilsson.

Hanell buckled under Eskilsson's persistence. 'If you say so,' he said. 'Still, strange. My memory's playing tricks on me, it's probably the onset of Alzheimer's.'

'Undoubtedly.'

'Do you think so?' Hanell looked worriedly at Eskilsson.

'No, I don't think so.' Eskilsson smiled convincingly.

'No, I thought as much. Extremely clear-sighted of you. Extremely clear-sighted.'

Hanell squeezed the tennis ball with an increasing frequency. For a moment there was silence, and the synthetic sound of the ball being scrunched together and then expanding, scrunched together and expanding filled the room.

'You have substantial experience of top positions with various interest groups. Why does this role interest you? You would be able to get a job anywhere, from what I can understand.'

'It fascinates me, this hypochondria. It's somehow in the grey zone between… I don't know, you're different, quite simply. I see it as a major challenge. You've surely got a way to go? To really make a proper breakthrough?'

'That was diplomatically put. It is true, we are relatively invisible. But we make a big difference for a lot of people,

I have to say. We receive a huge number of letters of gratitude. And a number of questions too, from people who experience that they are not taken seriously by healthcare institutions. The other day I received a question from a member who had a swelling of the hallux. In that case we were able to recommend a good doctor for a consultation. That isn't something we would normally do, but we try to give the best advice possible.'

'What's it like giving advice when you yourselves are so deeply, how should I put it, pessimistic?'

'Realistic,' corrected Hanell. 'If there is a ninety-nine percent chance that the condition is harmless, you'll think that you can rule out the worst. But in my world, one percent is one percent, no more or less. That is the difference between you and me. The problem is that there are lots of one percents. One percent MS here, three percent leukaemia there. You quickly end up over a hundred percent.'

'Is that a realistic way to look at it, do you think?'

'Statistics are statistics. There's nothing I can do about it,' said Hanell. 'But in any case. You see this mission as a challenge? What would you do to put hypochondria on the map?'

'There are many options. It's about patience, I think. And I would probably want to get a feel for the organisation before giving suggestions for drastic action.'

'Do you not have any ideas already now?' Hanell put the ball down and rubbed at his wrist.

Eskilsson felt his way forward. 'I think that you should be working with a real focus on parliament. Maybe educating caregivers in what hypochondria actually involves. Because I understand from you that there is a lack of knowledge.'

'Exactly. Very good,' said Hanell. He lowered his voice. 'But I should tell you what I think I've ended up with. For real.' He looked distraught.

'Yes?' said Eskilsson.

'Carcinoma. Cancer, as you laypeople say. Of the pancreas.' He stroked his belly.

'What makes you think that?' said Eskilsson.

'Nothing really. That's the problem. The sinister thing about this illness is that you're completely asymptomatic for a long time. And that's just what it's like, I feel absolutely healthy, have done for much longer than usual. I don't have any symptoms. Yet. Apart from that thing with my nuts.'

'But you can't look at it like that?' said Eskilsson. He looked around. 'That's the same as if I pointed at that chair and said that if there was an invisible cat there, then the chair would look empty. The chair looks empty – therefore there's an invisible cat sitting on it!'

Hanell's expression contorted in fear. He flew up out of his seat, jumped up and stood on it.

'Oh Jesus, oh Jesus.' He was hyperventilating. 'To think that I've never thought of that. Get it out! Get it out!'

'Take it easy,' said Eskilsson. 'That's exactly what I was trying to say, that you can't reason like that.'

'Out! Out! Schoo!' Hanell grabbed a large pencil sharpener, one of those with a crank, and threw it at the chair but missed. 'I'm not sitting down again before you've made sure that it's gone.'

Eskilsson sighed and went over to the chair, slowly. 'Sch, sch, sch,' he reached out his hand, crept forward. With a swift movement, he grabbed the invisible cat.

'Have you got it?'

'Yes, I've got it! Can you open the door?'

Hanell went past Eskilsson and the cat sideways with his back to the wall, the whole time with an eye on the invisible beast which was apparently trying to escape from Eskilsson's grasp. Hanell lifted his foot and kicked the door handle so that the door opened. Eskilsson carried the cat out, put it down outside, backed into the room again and quickly shut the door. They sat down again.

'I hate cats. Thank you for your quick thinking,' said Hanell. 'How long can it have been sitting there, do you think?'

Eskilsson shrugged. 'A week, tops.'

'A week? Good grief! But not longer, right?'

'No, not longer, I wouldn't have thought so.'

'Sure?'

'Sure.'

Hanell started laughing, relieved that the danger had been averted. Then he pointed at Eskilsson. 'You should have seen your scared face when you caught it! Haha!'

Esikilsson also forced out a laugh. Hanell reached his hands out in a cat catcher gesture and tried to look terrified. 'Sch, sch, sch, hahaha!' He breathed out, 'Dear, oh dear… no I really shouldn't laugh at you. I have a certain understanding for how it could have been unpleasant. I was also a little on edge if I'm honest.'

'Were you really?' said Eskilsson, not without irony.

'It was mainly that it was so unexpected.'

'Yes.'

'It's a good quality, that,' said Hanell and pointed at Eskilsson. 'That you have the ability to see things that are not entirely obvious. You've really got your head screwed on.'

'Thanks.'

'You'll be important here. Where were we?'

'You were talking about being asymptomatic.'

Hanell immediately looked crestfallen. 'Oh. Yes, right. I maybe have a year left, possibly two. I just wish I could achieve something of value in that time.'

'I'm sure you have plenty of good years left.'

Hanell laughed sarcastically. 'Yeah, right. Your optimism is really infectious. Infectious like Ebola.' He softened his tone. 'Which is of course a terrible illness,' he muttered and made a note.

He took a napkin out of a dispenser on the table and blew his nose, blowing several times before he moved the tissue away from his face and studied its contents. First from a distance, then up close. 'But what the hell?' he whispered. His eyes were only centimetres from the tissue, he looked like he was trying to read the smallest print on a bank note. Without folding the tissue together, he laid it on the table, with the contents facing up, slid open a desk drawer and pulled out a square, white metal box with a red cross on. He took the lid off and started to dig around in the box, took out a nasal spray, held it in front of himself and stared at it. Looked at the snotty paper on the table, then back at the spray again. He sighed and put it back in the box, continued to root around until he found a new nasal spray, a smaller bottle this time, in lighter material.

He read the label for a few seconds, took the stopper out and pressed twice in each nostril, put the spray back, the lid on and the box back in the desk drawer.

Eskilsson had been studying Hanell's ritual. 'What's wrong?' he asked.

'Oh, no, nothing, probably. Nothing at all. Haha.' His laugh seemed mainly intended to be for the purpose of calming Hanell himself.

'Can I ask you something?' said Eskilsson. 'What is it you are afraid of, really, I mean? Deep down?'

'Afraid?' said Hanell.

'Yes. You're afraid of dying, I assume? A hypochondriac is presumably never afraid of getting, I don't know, a common cold, for example? It's always serious illnesses that you are worried about?'

'We all have to walk that path. There is nothing strange about that,' said Hanell and folded his arms. He looked past Eskilsson.

'Yes, everyone has to die. Do you struggle to accept that?'

'Are you a psychologist?' asked Hanell. 'Kent Eskilsson, authorised psychologist. You should have a name badge like that.'

'I am actually a trained therapist, but that's not why I'm asking.'

'Well, well,' said Hanell, still with his arms folded. He rocked in his chair.

'I'm just trying to learn a bit about you. If I am going to work for your organisation, I want to get some insight into how you operate.'

'Good. That's positive,' admitted Hanell unwillingly. 'And of course, I have had a luxated left patella a few times and that, I can tell you, hasn't given me any major concerns, even if the pain was intense. So you do perhaps have a point with that about... you know.'

'Death?'

'Call it what you will.'

'Then I'll call it death.'

'Yes, yes, yes,' Hanell said and waved his hand.

'What's it like when others talk about their symptoms? Do you see such severe implications with them as you do with your own ailments? Or can you look at it more objectively?'

'As I said, I always look at the situation objectively. One percent is one percent. Ten percent is ten percent. It's really quite incredible that anyone is alive at all, when you think about all the dangers around every corner.'

'Yes. But the question is what is worst, to fear the thousands of ways in which you can die, or to actually die in one of those ways,' said Eskilsson.

'That sounds like a quote.'

'It probably is,' said Eskilsson and smiled.

Hanell deepened his voice to sound like a man in a movie trailer. 'Kent Eskilsson. Authorised psychologist *and* philosopher.'

Eskilsson looked troubled.

'No, no,' said Hanell, 'don't take it the wrong way, it was well-meant. I like it.'

'Thank you.'

But he couldn't stop himself. 'The philosopheeer!' he boomed with an abyssal voice. He stood up and pretended to shoot an m/45 in slow-motion, his body shaking from the force of the violent weapon. 'G-g-g-g-g-g! The philosopheeer.' He plucked an imaginary hand grenade from his waist, pulled out the pin with his teeth and threw the grenade, all in slow-motion. A few seconds later the grenade exploded and sent shockwaves through the room. Hanell collapsed down into his chair, as if dead.

'Yes, yes, yes,' said Eskilsson. 'I get it.'

'No offence,' laughed Hanell when he came round from his war injuries.

'It's fine,' said Eskilsson. 'I understand that you struggle to be serious when you're talking about these matters. Getting to the root of the problem. At an abstract level, it works, life and death and sickness, but when we get to talking about you, it becomes harder. It's absolutely fine.'

Hanell started to stroke his wispy beard and repeated Eskilsson's words with an even voice. 'Get to the root of the problem. Be serious. Life and de-ath.' He laughed. 'Chill out a bit, Freud.'

Eskilsson shook his head and smiled. 'It's absolutely fine as far as I'm concerned. From my perspective, I can say that I would be happy to work with you. Even if you are a bit crazy. Or maybe because of that. I think I'm needed here.'

'Never was a truer word spoken!' said Hanell. 'We've long been looking for a philosopher. Someone who can show us the truth, an enlightened individual. A Plato, a Hegel, a… I don't know any more philosophers.'

'Kant? Nietzsche?'

'A Kant, a Nietzsche! That's what we are after.'

Eskilsson continued shaking his head. Hanell went quiet. 'You will have to learn to put up with us,' said Hanell, back to being serious. 'I appreciate your honesty. We all have our problems here. But who doesn't? Everyone is crazy when you start to dig a little.'

'You're probably right.'

Hanell stroked his paunch. 'I'll put this to the board and hopefully you'll get an answer within a week. The sooner you can start, the better.'

'Good. I can probably start straight after the New Year,' said Eskilsson and got up.

Hanell moved as if to get up but suddenly went white in the face. He pointed in front of him, his eyes wide.

'The chair!' he shouted. 'It still looks empty!'

Also by Nordisk Books

Havoc
Tom Kristensen

*You can't betray your best friend
and learn to sing at the same time*
Kim Hiorthøy

Love/War
Ebba Witt-Brattström

Zero
Gine Cornelia Pedersen

Termin
Henrik Nor-Hansen

Transfer Window
Maria Gerhardt

Inlands
Elin Willows

Restless
Kenneth Moe